KILLING GRINDS

ORCHARD HOLLOW 3

A.N. SAGE

OLIVERHEBERBOOKS

CONTENTS

CHAPTER 1

Bright blue electricity coursed through the air and bounced off the walls. I ducked down, shielding my head with a plastic popcorn bowl as I swerved right and left to avoid the bursts of energy loose in my kitchen. My heart thundered in my chest, and I could feel its rising beat behind my temples. This was an epic disaster.

"Get a grip!" Stella, my ghost familiar, shouted from her hiding spot behind the couch. "You're going to kill us all at this rate!"

I growled low in my chest. "You're already dead!" I yelled back. "And why are you hiding? My magic can't hurt you. Come over here and help."

Grudgingly, my ghost familiar pulled herself from

the non-threatening terror she faced and floated toward me. Her sheer body glitched a few times to let me know she wasn't pleased being this close to my out-of-control magic. *That makes two of us, girlfriend.* When Stella was near enough, I gestured to a large amethyst chunk sitting on the kitchen counter six feet away from me. "Throw that my way, would you?"

Stella rolled her eyes, but obliged. Her gray physique shimmered as she vanished, only to reappear beside the crystal. Eyes closed tightly, Stella murmured under her breath and wrapped her see-through fingers over the crystal. I sucked in a breath and held it, knowing that to interrupt Stella while she was attempting to interact with the physical world meant a certain death.

A whooshing sound pierced the air, and I threw my hand up to catch the crystal. It bounced off my palm, landed on the floor, and rolled a few feet until it hit the barstool leg beside me.

"Great catch," Stella drawled. "You must have been a blast in gym class."

"Will you give it a rest, please? We have bigger fish to fry over here."

I reached for the amethyst and cradled it to my chest. The bowl tipped on my head and covered my eyes and I didn't bother righting it. Having less sensory stimulation right now was better. My chest rose and fell as I tried to steady my breathing, using the crystal as a conduit to gain control of my magic. It was an old trick Gran taught me when I was too young to understand the consequences of witch magic. When in trouble, find an external energy source and use it to dampen your power. Crystals were always a good bet since the ones witches used were dug out from the earth closest to the ley lines. And the crystals Gran had on hand were often spelled to amplify their energies, so I was pretty certain the amethyst would do the trick.

Body settling into a familiar state of control, I rocked back and forth, feeling for the power in the crystal. My fingertips tingled, and I smiled. "Got ya!"

Not wasting more time, I held on to the crystal's energy while reaching for my wild magic wreaking havoc on the kitchen. Goosebumps spread over my arms and I felt a few sparks burst on the tips of my fingers. Using my free hand, I pushed my palm out, directing it at the electricity bouncing off a set of pots on the stovetop. The magic stopped mid-air and changed direction, barreling toward my outstretched hand.

"Incoming!" Stella cried out as the electric current jumped into my body.

The force of it was so strong it sent me gliding

across the floor, my back colliding with the refrigerator. "Ooof!" I groaned. "That was rough."

"Your choice of headwear is rough," Stella sniped. "That was a catastrophe."

I dropped the amethyst and reached atop my head to remove the bowl I was still sporting. Dusting off my jeans, I took stock of the mess that was the kitchen. There were scorch marks on every surface and several dishes lay in a broken pile on the floor, having met their final end. "This is going to take forever to clean up."

A scurry of tiny feet sounded upstairs, followed by the unmistakable sound of an object breaking. I slapped my forehead. "For the love of! Harry!"

My annoyance was met with chitters and more raccoon footsteps from the upper level of the farmhouse. It had been weeks, and I was yet to find a way to get Harry Houdini, our resident raccoon and rascal, out of the house. If I waited any longer, I'd have to admit that I somehow managed to not only fill the house Gran left me with a snobby ghost, but a feral animal to boot. No matter how you looked at it, life in Orchard Hollow was far from boring. I really thought that after the near-death experience I had when I got in the middle of yet another murder, things might settle down. Instead, they only became more complicated.

My magic, which wasn't witch magic at all, was not one I understood. To make matters worse, the fact that my power had some sort of connection to Hades and the underworld was starting to feel like a reality. As Stella pointed out, it would explain why I had a ghost familiar instead of a proper cat like every other witch in town.

Then there was the question of my birth father, or "M" as we have come to know him based on some old letters he wrote to my mom. I still had no idea how to find the man or where to start looking. It would be so much easier if I could simply ask my wayward mother, but of course she up and disappeared on me not long before Gran died.

And that dumpster fire wasn't even my biggest concern.

I glanced at Stella's scowl as she tracked Harry's footsteps echoing upstairs. "I think we need to make a list of everything you remember," I told her.

Before we got tied to one another, my familiar found herself on the opposite side of the living without any memory of how she got there. Up until recently, she wanted nothing to do with figuring out what happened to her, and I respected her choice and stayed out of it. Imagine my surprise when Stella Rutherford not only decided she was ready to face the fireworks, but needed my help to do it.

Was I worried that if we figured out how Stella died that she'd poof her stuck-up butt from this world and I'd lose one of my closest friends? Sure. But I had to help her. Stella deserved to know what happened to her and as much as I hated to admit it, I had a bit of a knack for all things murder.

"I already told you everything I know," Stella said, pulling me away from my thoughts. The tennis outfit she died in swished as she brushed a ghostly hand over the short skirt, her long ponytail swaying from side to side behind her. Somehow, even in death Stella managed to appear put together. Though that likely had a lot to do with all the work the woman had done before she bit the dust. In case anyone was wondering, ghosts can have lip injections too. Odd.

I frowned. "It's not much. All you said was you think it wasn't an accident. I can't very well call the sheriff with a hunch from a ghost, can I? We need more."

"Well, I don't know what to tell you," Stella replied. "I don't have more. If I did, don't you think—"

Her eyes glassed over and she looked past my shoulder into nothingness. Trying to get her to snap out of her daze, I waved a hand in the air and blew out a breath into her face. Nothing. Whatever caught Stella's attention had her hooked. She'd been having these strange occurrences more often in the last couple of days and while it was absolutely unnerving to see, she usually got right back to business moments after. At first, her space-outs freaked me the heck out, but Stella assured me it was nothing more than her way of dealing with the missing pieces of her memory. Like she needed to buffer for a bit to dig deep into the things she'd forgotten. The explanation didn't ease my mind, but what could I do? Take her to see a ghost doctor?

Leaving Stella to her horror-movie-level experience, I turned my back to the ghost and concentrated on cleaning up the kitchen. On the counter, my phone vibrated, and I grabbed it before it plummeted to the floor.

Butterflies fluttered in my belly as the hope of Joe texting filled my heart. The new bookshop owner and I were yet to go on the date we'd been talking about for ages. Between Stella's situation, my magic, and Bean Me Up—the cafe I owned—something constantly came up.

I looked at the screen, deflating when I saw Cilia's name pop up. Sliding the call to answer, I pressed it to my ear and tried to shake off my disappointment. "Hi, Cilia."

"Hey, Addison. What are you doing this Friday?" The witch asked.

I mentally checked my wide-open schedule, saying, "Nothing after I close the cafe. Why?"

"The girls and I are meeting up for drinks. You should join."

If by "the girls" she meant her coven mates, I so was not interested. Cilia was actually a great person, and we had become quite close lately, but I was yet to bond with her other friends. Mostly because they were all witches in a coven led by my nemesis, Nancy Steeles.

As if reading my mind, Cilia sighed on the other end of the line. "Don't worry, Nancy won't be there. It'll be fun, trust me."

"Um...okay," I breathed out. "What's the worst that can happen?"

I knew better than to say that by now. As soon as I uttered the words, Stella's eyes fluttered and refocused, her pupils dilated as she emerged from the trance. I creased my brow. "Cilia, I have to call you back," I said, hanging up. Turning my full attention to my familiar, I took a few steps to close the distance between us. "Everything all right?"

"Sort of," Stella said solemnly.

"Did you...?"

She waved her hand to dismiss me. "Nope. Nothing new to report."

"Darn. You were gone a while. I really thought you remembered more this time."

"I didn't," Stella said. "But something has been gnawing at me. I know I woke up in the woods and I was—" she ran a hand over her fit body "—this way. So it stands to reason I died there. But why would I be in the middle of nowhere that early in the morning?"

I scratched my head. "You were a jogger, right? You must have been running on the trails when," I carefully selected my words, "it happened."

"I don't know. Jogging before a session of tennis seems wildly intense even for me."

My gaze rolled over the tennis skirt she sported, and I pursed my lips. I simply assumed Stella worked out like a mad woman to keep her perfect physique, but she had a point. Why would she go jogging before hitting the courts? Being tired would muck up her game and if there was one thing I knew about Stella Rutherford, it was that she was dead serious about tennis. No pun intended.

"Hmm," I mused. "You might have a point. Tell you what, help me clean this up and I'll make a stop at the library to see if I can dig anything up in the newspaper archives before work. Your death might have been a story they covered."

"Darling, please," my familiar mused. "I am a Rutherford. Of course, there will be a story."

Rolling my eyes, I flung a dishtowel her way, and it ripped through her body, landing on the floor behind her. "Watch it," Stella warned.

I pointed to the coffee spill on the floor next to her foot. "I'll watch it after you wash it. Put those new tricks of yours to good use and pull some weight around here." I grinned devilishly. "Or Harry stays forever."

Stella's hand shot up defensively and she bent down, her ghostly hand picking up the rag. "When you put it that way," she said, before rubbing at the coffee stain.

We spent the next half hour tidying up the place. When we finished, I thanked Stella, finger-brushed my hair into a messy bun, and headed out the door. If I left now, I'd have just enough time to hit the library right when they opened. Despite what Stella believed, I wasn't so sure I'd find anything useful in the archives, but it was worth a shot. At least we were moving forward.

Foot on the gas, I sped out of the driveway and headed into town, a renewed sense of hope rushing through me.

CHAPTER
2

The Orchard Hollow library sat at the end of a dead-end street and was nestled between two large oaks that obscured most of it from view. Much like the town itself, unless you knew where to go, you might have missed the place all together. When I was little, Mom used to bring me here when I became too rowdy and full of toddler energy. I remembered the awe I felt as I stepped foot through the front doors: a new world unfolding before my eyes.

I wound the car around the building and parked in the tiny lot belonging to the library. Double checking that I brought my library card, I noted the time—a half hour until I had to leave—and made my way to the entrance.

Entering the library as a grown-up held little of the same magic it did when I was younger. The air smelled of dust and mold and there were so many shelves of books filling the small Victorian building; it was claustrophobic. I thought back to Brooks Books, Joe's shop, and missed the place instantly. It was so much more organized than where I found myself now.

A throat cleared to my right, and I stumbled, bumping against a rolling cart with a stack of books on its top level. The books wobbled, and I held my breath, praying I didn't destroy public property before I had a chance to do what I came here to do. When the cart steadied, I blew air out through my clenched teeth and turned around.

Behind a wide mahogany desk sat an ancient-looking woman. She wore thick-rimmed gold glasses and had two pens sticking out of a graying bun. I wasn't a hundred percent sure, but I had the distinct feeling this woman may have been the librarian when I was a kid.

Her eyes narrowed on me and she tapped a finger on a small metal box. "Card, please," she instructed.

I dug into my pocket and held out my library card, waving it under the scanner to check in. Waiting for further instruction, I stayed put, but the woman lost interest in me immediately. I bit down on my tongue to keep my smart-ass remarks to myself and scurried into the belly of the building.

Around me, wood shelves sprouted from the floor and reached the ceiling. At this hour of the day, I was the only person here, and I looked around, noticing how creepy the place truly was. I doubted the library got much use and could finally understand why mom hated coming here so much. There were way better places to spend your time in while in Orchard Hollow.

Choosing the least cluttered aisle, I trudged toward the rear of the library where the computers were set up. When I emerged from the dusty passage, my mood brightened. It seemed the library was hiding its best feature all the way back here.

Before me, vast floor-to-ceiling windows lined the rear wall and comfy chairs sat around low tables in clusters. Beyond the windows, the dense trees of the forest provided a mystical view. My feet stepped on the world's softest rug and I felt myself melt into its embrace. It even smelled different in this section, like a fresh morning after a summer rain.

This must have been a newer addition to the building.

I wove around the chairs and headed straight for the row of desks in the far left corner. Most were stocked with the newest computers, but at the end, there was an old microfiche reader gathering dust inside a wooden vestibule. The local paper's archives only dated as far back as a year on their website and when I enquired about earlier copies, they pointed me here. As I pulled out a chair to sit down, I tried not to laugh. It was as though I had stepped through a time loop. I powered on the machine and it came to life with a clicking noise loud enough to wake the dead. Grinding my teeth to pulp, I waited for eons until it was ready to go and started my search. My fingers rolled the side wheel impatiently, trying to find the newspaper issue dating back to Stella's death.

I made it as far as the year it happened when hushed whispers interrupted my concentration. I couldn't make out every word, but a few jumped out. My name, specifically.

Craning my neck to peer around the vestibule's walls, I held my breath and listened in.

"I heard she's chasing after him like a hungry puppy," a woman whispered.

My blood boiled. Nancy-freaking-Steeles. What was she even doing here at this hour? While I missed the entire first half of the conversation, it was abundantly clear she was gossiping with someone about me and Joe, the new to town bookshop owner who happened to be my sort of possibly boyfriend. Or at least someone I was starting to date. Joe also happened to be a vampire but we didn't talk about that with others; paranormals liked to coast under the radar, even amongst their own kind.

Listening in, my hands fisted, and I fought the urge to stomp over and punch Nancy's lights out.

"Really?" the other woman asked, a coven mate, most likely. "They seemed pretty chummy to me last I saw them."

Nancy sighed so loud I was surprised the librarian didn't scold her. "Oh, please. Piper has no shot with him. He's probably waiting until he can let her down easy." She said something else I didn't quite catch, then added, "You know, I'm pretty sure her mother left because she couldn't handle being around her. I mean, come on! Having a daughter with such pathetic magical abilities in that powerful family must be embarrassing."

My body shook, and I pushed away from the table, standing on wobbly feet. My palms were slicked with sweat and I felt my magic rise to the surface. Electricity sparked on my skin and my eyes widened as I prepared to show Nancy exactly how wrong she was.

Footsteps sounded near to where the gossip queen stood, and they grew louder quickly. Then another voice broke up the silence of the library.

"There you are," a familiar tone said.

Nancy huffed out an annoyed breath. "Well, what do you know? It's Piper's fan club."

"Give it a rest," Cilia sniped, coming to my defense. "Your jealousy is showing."

"Me? Jealous of Piper? You're kidding, right?"

I could hear Cilia chuckle and pictured her stoic face. Pictured her tucking her long bob of blonde hair behind her ears as she got ready to tell Nancy off; she was always good at standing up for herself, despite what I originally pegged her as. For the longest time, I thought of Cilia as one of Nancy's brainless minions, but she'd proven me wrong. Cilia Craven was a witch you didn't want to mess with and I started to wonder if she would have made a better leader for their coven than Nancy.

"You know, Nance," Cilia said, "if you spent as much time on yourself as you do on spreading rumors, you might have a better time." Though I couldn't see them, I was certain Nancy's face must have been beet-red with anger. I could all but hear her head explode when Cilia added, "And last I heard, your marriage isn't exactly the epitome of romantic success."

Ladies and gentlemen, we have ourselves a winner! Everyone knew Nancy and her husband, who happened to be my high-school boyfriend, had a marriage of convenience. It was your standard tale. Girl meets boy. Girl gets pregnant. Girl and boy get married and spend the rest of their lives miserable and very much out of love. If Nancy wasn't such a devil, I'd have felt sorry for her.

"Ugh, whatever," the witch remarked. "I forgot you're besties with the magical wasteland. I have to go anyway. See you at the ritual tonight."

Their retreating steps echoed through the library and I heard the door swing open, then shut. My shoulders slumped, and I wiped the sweat off my brow, relieved when I noticed my magic slink back into my body. Blowing up the town's library with my weird brand of power was not going to make the rumors any better.

I shook off the last few minutes and lowered back down to sit, my eyes scanning the screen again. As I flicked the pages, I caught a glimpse of Stella's name and stopped.

"Here we go."

Zooming in on the article, I read through it quickly, which wasn't hard to do since it was barely a mention. It seemed Stella's assumption that her death would drive in the media was dead wrong. The only thing the article revealed was her name, and that she was found at the bottom of a cliff not far from one of the hiking trails in the woods.

My eyes narrowed on the last passage. "Why would you go jogging on a hiking trail?"

I wasn't much for exercise, but even I knew that it sounded quite odd. The Orchard Hollow woods were rough terrain on a good day. Most tourists who came through often said that hiking on our trails was the toughest physical activity they had endured. Despite the difficulty of getting through the wildness, we had a few weirdos in town who enjoyed running—a task I was allergic to—and the town had no choice but to make their life easier. I was about ten years old when they blocked the woods off and dug out trails and roads to add more accessible passages for those who wanted to run. And not because someone was chasing them.

So why was Stella not found on one of those roads? How did she end up at the bottom of a cliff, of all places?

I made a mental note to ask her if she enjoyed hiking and turned off the microfiche machine. Checking the antique clock on the wall, I rushed to the front door and bolted to the parking lot. It was a twenty-minute drive to Cliff Row, the main street in town, and I had ten minutes until the cafe was to open. Cursing my poor sense of time, I hauled myself into the Beetle and started her up. I was late. Again.

Rory was going to kill me.

CHAPTER 3

My assistant glared at me over shiny, pink sunglass frames shaped like daisies. Today, Rory's hair was tied into two space buns, and I noticed a new addition of a purple streak running up one side. Her signature attire of pastel goth stood out like a sore thumb on the early morning landscape of Cliff Row. As I approached, Rory's lips puckered, and she lowered the sunglasses down the bridge of her nose to see me clearer.

"If you're going to be late all the time, can I come in at like ten instead?" Rory asked.

"Sorry!" I offered, fumbling for the door keys in my purse. When I finally got it open, I let her push past me to get inside. "I had something important to check on and lost track of time. It won't happen again."

Rory arched one eyebrow. "Right. So...ten then?"

"We open at eight," I said. "So no. But I'll buy you lunch to make up for having to wait."

Despite the annoyed sigh my assistant let out, she walked to the coffee bar and grabbed her apron off the hook, tying it around herself tightly. My eyes caught the bedazzled spaceship logo on the front—a new addition.

"I like what you did with it," I said, smiling warmly.

Rory shrugged. "Needed to pass the time. It's not a big deal."

I didn't bother telling Rory that if she was bored on her shift, she could stock the baked goods display or clean up the messes she often left behind. Since I already started the morning pissing off the teenager, there was no point ruining the rest of the day by getting on her bad side. If I knew anything about teen girls, it was best to leave them alone until they had some food and coffee. Kind of like bears.

Leaving Rory to her moping and attitude, I skirted around the counter and started up the espresso machine. It roared to life and soon the sweet, delicious smell of burning beans and warm milk filled the cafe. We worked in separate parts of the space as we did every morning, each of us getting their own areas up to snuff in time to open the doors. In the last few months that Rory worked for me, she really stepped up her game. While she continued to spill pretty much every second coffee—a staple move of hers—I knew I could trust her to watch the cafe if I had to step away. It was really nice to have help for once.

I watched Rory dust the space-themed figurines on the one of the shelves above the seating area before moving to arrange fresh flowers on the bar spanning the main window. The young witch moved fluidly, her head bopping along to a song playing on her headphones.

I smiled, grateful for her presence on this particular day. The article on Stella's death rattled me and I couldn't get the image of my familiar lying at the bottom of a cliff out of my head.

"Why were you even there, Stella?"

"What was that?" Rory yelled, one headphone out of her ear.

I waved her off. "Talking to myself! Ready to open?"

As she nodded, I walked over to the front door and peered outside. There was already a small queue of customers waiting for their morning coffee. I wiped my brow, flipped the "closed" sign over, and unlocked the door, hoping that the morning rush will keep thoughts of Stella out of my fraying mind.

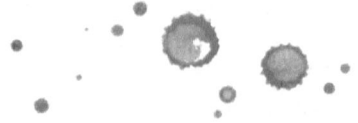

The rush did indeed keep me busy enough that Stella's name barely flashed in my mind. By the time the last of the regulars got their coffee—an apple spiced latte—I was out of breath and out of thoughts.

The bell above the door rang out and my eyes darted to the spaceship clock on the wall. Quarter to eleven, which could only mean one thing. Taking off my cinnamon stained apron, I kept my back to the door and said, "Hi, Joe."

A low laugh rumbled behind me and I spun around to face Joe Brooks, our new bookshop owner and very sexy vampire. Joe's wide-set shoulders flexed under the tight sweater he wore and he ran his fingers through his gray-dusted short hair, his green eyes glued to me.

"Am I that predictable?" Joe asked.

I sighed and placed the latte he usually ordered on the counter. "Not at all."

Joe laughed again and picked up the cup, inhaling the steam rising off the top. He would never actually drink it, vampire and all, but it helped his image to carry food and drinks around to throw people off the scent. Very few paranormals were open about their magical abilities in Orchard Hollow, despite how many of us lived here on account of the town sitting above a network of ley lines that amplified our powers. Still, the humans didn't need to know about magic. Not if history taught us anything.

"How's the morning treating you?" Joe asked. He reached into his jacket pocket as he spoke and pulled out a rectangle wrapped in brown paper. "Before I forget," he said and slipped the package into my hand.

I turned it around curiously, smiling at the ghost imprint on the front; Joe's store logo. "Which one is it this time?"

Since our discovery of my magic's background, Joe had taken it upon himself to be my personal research assistant. He scoured every inch of the bookstore he purchased after his uncle's death for anything that might point me in the right direction. Even went as far as ordering books in from other stores in the country, one of which I guessed I currently held in my hands.

"The Compendium of Ancient Magic," Joe answered. "Might be nothing, might be everything."

I smirked. "The usual, then?"

"Correct." Joe rubbed the back of his neck, the muscles of his biceps stretching the thin fabric of his jacket. I averted my eyes from the distraction immediately. "So, good morning so far?" Joe repeated.

"Actually..." I tipped my chin in the direction of the office, indicating for him to follow me. Once we were out of earshot of the patrons, I closed the door and said, "I think Stella was right."

"About?"

Geez, Piper. Use your words.

Leaning against the solitary desk in the office, I crossed my arms and gathered my thoughts, trying to remember how much I'd revealed of my familiar's unfamiliar afterlife. "Sorry, I forgot to tell you last time. Stella asked me to look into her death to see if I can figure out what happened to her."

Joe's thick eyebrow quirked. "I thought she couldn't remember anything."

"She can't, not really. But she doesn't believe she died by accident," I explained. "And I agree with her."

There was about an hour until the next rush and I didn't want to waste any time. I sucked in a breath and spilled everything I discovered at the library, little as it was. I made sure to leave out the part about Nancy's big mouth running all over town. There was no need to get Joe mixed up in that witch's drama. After I solved the mystery of Stella's death, I was going to put Nancy in her place once and for all. A rogue smirk pulled on my lips as I pictured checking off that item from my life goals list.

"And you're sure she didn't go for a jog and lost her balance?" Joe asked when I finished speaking.

I nodded. "One hundred percent. I've been on those trails; no one in their right mind would jog anywhere near the cliffs. If they found Stella at the bottom of one, it wasn't because of a jogging accident." Thinking back to the outfit my familiar was stuck in for the remainder of her ghostly life. "Plus, she was wearing her tennis clothes. She wasn't dressed to jog."

Leaning in closer, Joe licked his lips, his eyes gazing past my head in deep thought. My throat tightened. This close, I could smell the aftershave he used this morning. *Get a grip, woman. You're smelling his skin now?* Perhaps Nancy was right; I was acting like a proper stalker.

I leaned back to put some space between us as Joe said, "You know, you're becoming quite the detective. I'm impressed."

"I haven't gotten anywhere yet," I countered. "All I have is a hunch and the world's most vague newspaper article."

Oblivious to the burning heat in my stomach, Joe inched closer again. "From what I recall, your hunches are usually spot on."

I have a hunch for something else right about now...

"Do you now?" Joe asked, grinning.

Oh, sweet mother of...I said that out loud. My cheeks were on fire and cold sweat beaded at the base of my neck, my hair clinging to it in clumps. This was it. This was how I was going to ruin my shot with the vampire before we even had a chance to start. To my absolute bewilderment, Joe didn't run straight for the door.

Instead, he closed the distance between us, his lips an inch away from mine. My breath hitched and excitement ripped its way through my body. I closed my eyes, parting my lips slightly to welcome the kiss.

Ice cold air rushed over face and I shivered, goosebumps spreading all over my arms and legs. My stomach tightened and bile filled my gut, rising to my throat. What was happening? I had the distinct feeling that I was about to retch, and panic overcame me. *Am I allergic to Joe?*

My eyes snapped opened, and a scream expelled from my lips as I saw the face before me. My head spun. I tried to find Joe in the office, spotting him a few feet away from me. My panic was quickly replaced with rage. "What the hell, Stella?!" I screeched. "Did you seriously manifest inside both of us?" I turned my attention away from the ghost to look at Joe. "Are you okay?"

He shook off the residual ghost energy that

coursed through his body with a shudder. "I'm good. A little warning next time would be great."

"You hear that?" I asked Stella. "We need to have a conversation about boundaries."

The ghost didn't register my words. Her gray physique shimmered and glitched, the look on her face telling me she wasn't bothered by her unbelievably poor timing. "That wasn't fun for me either, you know," she said.

"Then stop doing it."

"How was I supposed to know you were getting some action in here?" my familiar asked. "You haven't had the guts to make a move on the bloodsucker for months."

"I am so over—"

Stella held up a transparent hand, shushing me. "You can scold me later," she said. "Right now, you need to get to the police station."

My throat closed up, and I looked between her and Joe. What was so urgent that she had to interrupt a perfectly wonderful moment, and why the heck did it involve the police? My first thought was that something happened at the house, but then Stella would have opened with that. Even if it had to do with Harry Houdini. No, this was different, and it had her up in a tizzy.

Peeling my gaze from Joe's questioning eyes, I

turned back to the ghost. "What's at the station that you need me to do? I'm in the middle of work if you haven't noticed."

Stella scoffed. "I'd hardly call that work," she teased. "I need you to grill Romero on my case."

It's official: Stella lost it.

"We already talked about this," I said. "The sheriff wasn't even on the force in Orchard Hollow when you died. He wouldn't be able to help, even if he wanted to. Which I doubt he would, by the way."

"Wrong, wrong, wrong," Stella sang. "I don't know where you're getting your information, but the sheriff was definitely on the force. You have to get him to reopen the case."

"And how do you know that?" I quizzed.

Stella rolled her big eyes and pursed her lips. "Because I saw him there," she said. "After I died. Romero was in the woods. He was the cop on the scene when they found me."

My familiar grinned like she'd won the lottery. Behind her, Joe shrugged and raised his hands, beckoning me to fill him in. Meanwhile, my butt sank into the desk and my stomach dropped. Stella's flash of memory should have made me more excited and yet all I could feel was nerves and discomfort.

The last time I asked the sheriff to open an old case, it didn't exactly go over well. In fact, despite

being in the loop about our town's paranormal presence, he didn't exactly enjoy talking about magic.
Every time I brought it up, I could see his entire body
tense like I had just informed him the black plague
was returning. Granted, in his defense, the previous
cold case I asked him to look into involved a death in
the most prominent hotel in town and led to me almost
getting my head blown off by a psycho killer.

No matter how much I wished to explain that this
time my nosiness had a reason, I doubted the sheriff
would care, even if he did previously ask for my
continuous help with cases involving our town's non-
human inhabitants.

How was I supposed to explain why I was looking
into Stella's death? The woman died years ago and on
paper had no connection to me whatsoever.

As I stood in the office, knots twisted my gut and I
swallowed hard to keep myself from puking.

I had to tell Romero about my relationship with
Stella Rutherford. Knowing the sheriff, this would
blow up in my face big time. I could only hope I'd
avoid being a prime suspect this time around.

CHAPTER 4

The police station loomed on the horizon as I drove up, its front doors ajar and resembling the open mouth of a nightmare creature. It wasn't that the station was menacing, quite the opposite. Between the cobblestone pathway leading from the parking lot to the front entrance and the planters of flowers lining it, the place was a downright oasis. I supposed it was only a nightmare to me and anyone else paying an unwelcome visit.

I entered the reception lobby, eyes scanning the seats for the usual drunks sleeping off a night of boozing. Today, the blue chairs were empty, and the station seemed too quiet. Even for a small town where things that required policing rarely happened.

A grumble sounded down the hallway leading to the interrogation rooms, or offices as Romero called them, and I froze in my spot. My eyes swung to the empty front desk; I had half a mind to duck behind it before whoever was speedily making their way to the front appeared. What was wrong with me? I had no idea why I was acting like I did something wrong. All I needed was information that was open to the public. Nothing sinister about that.

I straightened my shoulders as the sheriff's wide-brimmed hat peeked around the doorframe. "Cassandra, can I get yesterday's—" Romero stopped in his tracks when he spotted me in the lobby, his lips forming a tight, thin line. "Miss Addison. What brings you by this morning?"

Translation: discover any bodies today, Piper?

I fixed the sheriff with the sweetest smile I could muster and took a step forward. "Hi, Sheriff. I was hoping I could ask you about an old case."

"Why is that?" Romero pinched the bridge of his nose and stared at his cowboy boots. His annoyance with me was quite clear this morning.

"It's for a friend," I explained. Then, looking around the reception area, added, "Probably best to talk somewhere private."

For a second, I thought the sheriff was going to tell me to take a hike. Imagine my surprise when Romero tipped the rim of his hat, turned on his heels, and marched back down the hallway he came from. He didn't say a word, and I assumed that meant I had little time before he changed his mind about speaking with me. Running after him, I bristled as he opened the door to an interrogation room, memories of me sitting in the same spot while the sheriff grilled me about a crime I didn't commit flashing through my system. I bristled, shaking off all of my discomfort, and took a seat opposite him at the sole table in the room.

Romero took off his hat and rested it between us. "Which case do you need information on, and why do you need it?" he asked. "And please, spare me no details, but make it quick."

Inhaling deeply, I met his fiery gaze and proceeded to word vomit for the next ten minutes. I told the sheriff about my odd familiar situation, keeping the part about the background on my magic to myself for now. From there, I explained Stella's amnesia and her insistence that her death was not an accident. I didn't fail to mention that I agreed with her because even though Stella wasn't here, I had her back. When I was done explaining, I ended the entire show with the bomb Stella dropped on me earlier. Somehow, Romero stayed quiet and had no reaction to my story, even when I told him that Stella remembered seeing him when she woke up as a ghost despite the fact that I was pretty certain he wasn't the sheriff then.

Finishing the world's fastest rendition of the mess that was my life, I folded my hands in my lap and peeked at Romero through my lashes. He didn't look angry, but most importantly, he didn't look like he wanted to have me committed. Score one for Piper!

"Let me see if I got all this," Romero said slowly. "Unlike most other witches in this town, your familiar is a dead woman who believes there was foul play involved in her death. Unfortunately, she can't remember anything except seeing me at the scene of the supposed crime. And you've taken it upon yourself to help her find out what happened, including but not limited to getting me to reopen a closed case from years ago. One that happened while I, as you yourself stated, was not even around for. Did I get it about right?"

I swallowed the hot lump in my throat. It tasted an awful lot like my pride. "Yep. That covers it," I said.

Romero brushed his forefinger over the comical mustache perching above his top lip. Unlike me and many of the town's residents, the sheriff was one hundred percent human. However, he was picked for the job because of his knowledge of the paranormal and his ability to look past our differences. At least, that's what I always thought. Romero and I weren't exactly best friends, though he did occasionally reach out to me when he needed help from someone in the magical community. An act he often seemed to regret.

"Miss Addison, I'm going to extend you the same courtesy I would give to any other coworker and be brutally honest," Romero said. *Coworker? Was I promoted?* "You are correct in thinking that I was not the town's sheriff when Mrs. Rutherford met her untimely end. I was, however, working with the Federal Bureau on another case, one that led me to Orchard Hollow and your friend."

My brain might have short-circuited because I could not formulate a sentence. Did Romero just tell me he was working on a federal case involving Stella? What case? And why her?

I rolled my shoulders and sat up ramrod straight in the chair. "Was Stella tied up in illegal dealings before she died?"

"I am not at liberty to reveal any information on federal cases to a civilian," the sheriff said. "Though I can tell you that your friend was not the object of my investigation."

I frowned. "Then who?"

Heat clawed its way up my body as I considered Stella's life before becoming my dead familiar. There wasn't much I knew about the debutante other than she married someone way too old for her. According to

Stella, it wasn't for the money and I believed her. Something about the way Stella spoke of her husband, or widower, told me she really loved the man. Despite his past wrong-doings, mainly those involving money laundering and a bit of jail time. If Romero was investigating someone close to Stella, it must have been her husband.

"Did your case have anything to do with Stella's husband?" I asked, convinced I already knew the answer.

The sheriff didn't reply, but I noticed the slightest nod. I kept pressing.

"Okay, I get it. You can't say anything. Can you at least tell me if you personally believe Stella's death was an accident?"

"Personally," the sheriff stated, "I don't think your friend was much of a hiker."

I nearly jumped out of my seat. "HA! You do think someone killed her!"

"Simmer down, Miss Addison," he drawled. "Here is what I can say freely. The case was open and shut; there was no evidence to convict anyone in your friend's circle as the responsible party for her death. The coroner ruled it an accident and since I had no jurisdiction in the town at the time, my hands were tied to investigate further. I will mention that from personal experience, when a death seems fishy, it often is. And it is often committed by those closest to the victim."

With that, the sheriff pushed his chair from the desk and walked to the door. He pointed to the hallway, indicating it was time for me to leave. Head bowed, I thanked him for his time and dragged myself out of the police station, piling into the Beetle with a disappointed huff.

My plan backfired.

Not only did Romero give me very little in the way of clues to further my search, but he pretty much told me that Stella's case was not going to reopen. I glanced out the window at the storm clouds gathering overhead, Orchard Hollow's rainy season rolling in fast. Stella would not like what I had to tell her when I got home tonight.

My mouth dried up.

She would enjoy the sheriff accusing her husband of her murder even less.

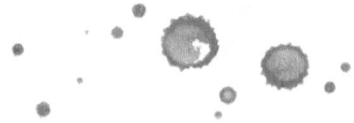

"Arthur didn't do it."

I rubbed my temples, the headache I was nursing exploding behind my lids. "Stella, for the twentieth

time, we have to at least check it out," I told my familiar. "Romero basically shoved me in your husband's
direction. I know it's not great, but you need to keep
an open mind."

"He. Didn't. Do. It."

Stella vanished and reappeared next to the
ottoman at the foot of my bed. Her teeth clamped
together, and I thought I heard her cuss seconds before
she kicked the ottoman with her foot. It skidded across
the floor and the screeching sound made the hair rise
on my arms. From inside my closet, Harry's angry chit-
tering ensued.

"Great! Now you pissed off the raccoon!" I yelled.
"Can you get yourself together? All I suggested was
that I talk to Arthur and see where it goes."

I was answered with another kick. This one was
higher and aimed at the cushion on my bed. The
cushion catapulted across the room and slammed into
the closet door. Inside, Harry was about to lose it,
which only meant one thing: my clothes would pay the
price for Stella's outburst.

"Stella! Knock it off!"

"I told you a million times to get rid of the rodent!"
she yelled back.

I knew better than to entertain her theatrics. Stella
was pissed off that I pointed the finger at her husband
and she was stubborn enough to bite my head off for it.

I wasn't at all intimidated by her, at least not the way I used to be before. Sure, Stella Rutherford was mighty scary when angered, but she didn't have a thing on my abilities.

The ghost raised her foot, her eyes set on the pile of clothes collecting dust near my bed. *That's it. I've had it.*

Not giving her a chance to move, I reached for my magic, aiming it close enough to the ghost to make a point. The electricity built inside me and thrummed at my fingertips. My eyes snapped open, and I spread my palms, slamming them outward in the direction I settled my gaze on. Deep down, my frustration built until I was barely able to hold it down.

The magic I set loose flashed as it barreled towards Stella. Before me, the ghost's eyes bulged and she let out a yelp, twisting to the right and away from my incoming attack. The magic hit the frame of the window behind her, sizzling as it ate through the wood. Stella scoffed, sticking her tongue out at me like a toddler.

"Will you please settle down now?" I asked.

"Only if you fix whatever that is."

My eyes followed Stella's extended finger all the way to the windowsill. The spot where my magic hit the frame was dark, and it appeared to be spreading. Fast.

Inching closer, I held my breath and reached for it.

"What are you doing?" Stella yelled at my back.

I blocked her out. My eyes narrowed to slits as I inspected the charred wood. The damage wasn't the same one my magic usually caused. Something was different about this; I couldn't figure out. The dark spot grew wider and, for a second, I thought I saw a flash of movement within it. Nose drawing closer to the remnants of magic, I took a few steps forward. The spot widened, almost like it was tearing through the surrounding air.

Slowly, my arm raised, and I pushed it toward the blackness, needing to touch it.

A sharp pain penetrated the flesh on my calf and I screamed, wobbling backward. The pain climbed up my leg and I stumbled, my butt hitting the mattress and making me tumble onto the bed. "Ow!" I yelled and looked down at my leg.

I caught a glimpse of Harry's furry behind as he scurried away from me to hide under the bed. On my calf, teeth marks formed a perfect circle. "Holy coffee bean!" I yelped. "He freaking bit me!"

"As much as I hate to admit it, I think he saved your witch butt," Stella said from the corner of the room.

I glanced her way, then back to the window. The strange rip was gone, leaving behind only a dark stain where my magic made contact with the wood. "What was that?"

"Who knows?" Stella shrugged. Helpful as usual. "You should definitely get that bite checked out. I don't think Cujo is up to date with his shots."

She started to disappear, then reformed again. "I meant was I said," Stella sniped, flipping her long ponytail over her shoulder. "Leave Arthur alone. He's been through enough."

Poof! She was gone.

Hobbling to the bathroom down the hall, I disinfected my calf and checked out the wound. Luckily, Harry didn't break the skin, and I was already noticing an improvement. The sucker was going to bruise, but there was a good chance I didn't get rabies. Winning!

Slapping a bandage over the fading wound, I headed back into the bedroom to clean up the mess Stella's tantrum left behind. My eyes stayed on the window frame, mind reeling. As much as I wanted to chalk up what happened to the odd behavior of my even odder magic, I wasn't so sure. Whatever that was, whatever I did, it felt intentional. If I didn't know any better, I'd say it felt like I opened some sort of doorway.

"Stop it," I scolded myself.

Magical doorways were a figment of the human

imagination. They were a thing of legends and myths, not anything rooted in real magic. And yet...I frowned.

Stranger things have happened in Orchard Hollow.

For once in my life, I hoped Nancy was right about me. *Please let me be a magical dud.* I had no time to deal with this, not when there was a murder to solve and a familiar to upset.

Looking around the bedroom to make sure I was alone, I pulled out my laptop and settled in. "Arthur Rutherford, let's see what we can find out about you."

CHAPTER 5

The few details listed online for Arthur Rutherford did not help me get to know the man one bit. If anything, by the time I clicked on a woman's profile that was a friend of a friend of a friend of Arthur's, I felt like a complete stalker.

The only information I could pinpoint was the short time he spent in prison for money laundering, though that happened when Arthur was much younger and wasn't news Stella didn't already share. It appeared that after the stint the man was on the straight and narrow path. At least he looked to be on paper.

I stared at a recent photograph of Mr. Rutherford

and scrunched my nose. He was so much older than Stella. I knew they had a good twenty years between them, but the guy was pushing eighty and Stella barely had a wrinkle to show for her fifty-plus years of age. Granted, that probably had to do with a certain sought after plastic surgeon in the city and the fact that she was dead. Ghosts didn't exactly age—a point Stella never forgot to mention every time I pulled out a gray hair.

Slamming the laptop shut, I let out a frustrated groan and crawled off the bed. At some point between my fight with Stella, getting mauled by a raccoon, and creeping a rich old guy online, the sun had set and night covered the front yard. I stifled a yawn, my growling stomach forcing me to abandon the comfort of my bed and head downstairs.

I slid the bedroom window open halfway for Harry to get out and grimaced. Did the raccoon live here now? Was I treating him as a pet? I really needed to find an alternate solution for the thieving critter soon.

Insides twisting with hunger, I skipped the last two steps and walked into the kitchen. In the dark of the evening, the place was sinister and gloomy and I had to still my racing heart when a branch knocked on the window above the sink. My fingers traced the outline of the light switch on the wall and I flicked it up.

Nothing happened.

I tried again, rattling the switch on and off and achieving the same unimpressive result. I flipped it again. What did they say about the definition of insanity? No matter.

Thunder boomed outside and a flash of lightning illuminated the kitchen. My eyes darted to the window, noticing the storm raging around me. Rain pelted the side of the house and it rattled my nerves to pieces. The thunder hit again, and I jumped.

"Great," I whispered to the empty farmhouse. "Storm must have taken out the lights again."

Living in a hundred-year-old farmhouse had its charm, but it was nights like this one that I wished I had a small apartment closer to civilization. At least there'd be neighbors to hear me scream if a chainsaw killer attacked.

I shook my head. No point scaring myself on top of everything else.

Taking a look at the front porch and the wetness gathering there, I opted to light the emergency candles instead of fiddling with the fuse box. If the last time the lights gave out taught me anything, it was that Gran didn't exactly have the wiring up to code in the house. Having an electrician in was on my to do list and I was cursing myself for not having done so sooner.

I decided to give the fuse box a look in the morning when the weather wasn't so wet and cold.

Using my phone to light the way, I gathered all the candles I stocked in a kitchen cupboard and arranged them throughout the downstairs. The farmhouse looked magical in the candle glow and if it weren't for the storm, this would have been a great night.

At least it was until my phone rang, startling me and making me trip over the arm of the couch. My legs buckled under me and I stutter-stepped sideways, knocking into the coffee table with a yelp. I rubbed my side. *That's going to bruise. Fabulous.*

"Hello?" I asked, answering the incessant ringing of the phone.

"Miss Addison, I'm glad I caught you."

My brow furrowed. "Sheriff Romero?" It was impossible to hide the surprise in my squeaky voice. "Anything I can help you with?"

"Quite the opposite," Romero said.

Another bolt of lightning hit and I screeched like an owl.

"Everything all right, Miss Addison?"

I swallowed my shame and said, "All good. You were saying you called to help me?" I was very confused, as per usual. "I don't think I follow."

"Look, I'm going to be completely frank with you," Romero stated. "As I mentioned earlier, my hands are tied with what I can tell you about Mrs. Rutherford's case. That said, I know you by now and I have the feeling you will not drop this no matter how much I wish you would."

He had a point.

"I'll make you a deal," the sheriff continued. "I will tell you what I can without pissing off the bureau and you give me your word that you will not get yourself into a foolish situation."

I assumed what Romero really wanted to say was, "I'll help you out but don't get yourself killed on my watch." Nodding to myself, I said, "Deal."

"I'll cut to the chase. When I told you my investigation with the bureau led me to Mrs. Rutherford, I didn't share the entire truth. My colleagues and I were working on a financial crimes case, one that was bigger than anything we encountered previously."

I choked on my own spit. "What did Stella have to do with it? Not sure if you know this, but she's not exactly a businesswoman. Or was. Whatever."

The sheriff cleared his throat on the other end of the line. "Since Mrs. Rutherford's husband was a known criminal, we were looking into him."

"Why him? I'm sure there were other people you

could have checked." His tale smelled like lies, and I didn't like it.

"The money laundering took place in several big name casinos and at the time had been going on for years."

Now it made sense. A casino. A financial crime. It had Arthur Rutherford's name written all over it since Arthur was convicted of money laundering before and conveniently owned the casino in town now. But Stella told me her husband went clean after he got caught the first time...unless she didn't know anything about it.

"We thought Mrs. Rutherford was in on it."

Oh.

I scratched my head and paced the length of the living room and back again. "That doesn't sound like Stella."

Romero sighed.

I grit my teeth together.

"You're right," he said. "As I worked the angles deeper, it became apparent that she had no idea what her husband was up to. I came to Orchard Hollow to convince her to go undercover and get information we could use to take down the money laundering ring."

My throat was bone dry and my vision spotted as I considered the sheriff's words. Blinking rapidly, I reached for a glass of water on the counter, then put it back down. "Did she agree to help?"

"I believe she would have," Romero answered, "but she died before I had a chance to broach the subject."

The way he said the last part gave me pause. I recalled the last hint the sheriff dropped in my lap in the station and froze. "You think Arthur found out and killed her before she could spill the beans?"

"Correct. The way in which your friend died, it was suspicious, yet there was no evidence to rule it a homicide. Convenient, wouldn't you say?"

"Definitely." My fingers were suddenly itchy, and I rubbed at them with my fingernails until they were blood-red. "Was there anything out of the ordinary when you found her?"

"I didn't find her," Romero corrected. "A tourist out for a hike called it in. When we arrived, Mrs. Rutherford was lying at the base of a cliff with all the signs of a fall as the cause of death. Except—"

His words trailed off, and I jumped in immediately. "Except what?"

"There was a fresh bruise around her wrist akin to a ligature mark. Since I couldn't find any abandoned restraints nearby I had no way to prove foul play. It always bothered me, though."

My tongue swelled in my mouth. I could see why

it would bother Romero. It was bothering me as well. Stella's death was becoming more and more extraordinary, and I wondered why Romero didn't push harder to keep the case open.

"A week after I arrived in Orchard Hollow, we caught a big break back in the city. The bureau was no longer interested in following Arthur Rutherford's trail and I was pulled away."

Well, that explained it.

I tightened my lips and asked, "And then you came back as the sheriff years later?"

"I did," Romero said. "I knew there was nothing I could do to find out what happened to your friend, not without stepping on the bureau's toes. But I thought maybe...maybe if I could help this town, I'd right a wrong somehow." He let out another deep sigh. "Then I found out about...your kind...and well, life went in a different direction."

It seemed that was a normal occurrence in our town. People often came here for one reason and ended up staying for another, though I wouldn't know since I'd lived here my entire life. I could almost hear Stella taking a jab at my sad existence, and it dragged me back to the conversation with the sheriff. I opened my mouth to speak, when my phone dinged with an incoming message. Joe's name flashed in a notification bar and my heart jolted.

"Thank you for telling me what you could," I told the sheriff. "I promise I won't share this with anyone."

"I'm more worried about what you'll do next, Miss Addison," Romero grumbled. "You have yourself a good night and stay inside if you can. It's wretched out there."

Glancing out the bay window, I bid the sheriff good night and promised to stay out of trouble. I may as well have crossed my fingers behind my back because now that I had a bone to chew on, I knew I would not rest until I got more information.

When the sheriff clicked off the line, I looked at my messages, the knots in my gut tightening when I scrolled down to Joe's last message.

My eyes crossed. "What...?"

The vampire's message made less sense than Harry Houdini on a bad day. I reread it, trying to decipher what he meant and coming up blank. After a few tries, I decided I was way too tired to keep going and called instead.

Joe answered on the first ring. "Hey, Piper. Got my message?"

"Sure did," I answered. "Does it come with a cipher code?"

Joe's deep laugh rumbled in my ear and I tried not to shiver from the way it made me feel. "I have a lead on your magic," Joe explained. "Hang on, let me send you a link. Want to meet tomorrow to go over it?"

The phone vibrated against my ear as Joe's second message came through. "Sounds good. Let's meet at Bean Me Up before I open if that's not too early."

"I'll be there," Joe murmured. "Stay warm tonight."

Cheeks hot as hell on fire, I clenched my teeth to avoid blurting out a ridiculous come back. When Joe hung up, I opened up the link he sent and read through it. My jaw gaped as I scrolled through the article. It appeared to be part of a thesis by an academic specializing in ancient magical lore.

"Well, will you look at that..." I whispered. It seemed I owed Joe a massive coffee to not drink tomorrow. He may have hit the jackpot.

CHAPTER 6

C offee and cinnamon swirled through the kitchen as I whipped up an apple spiced latte to go. The morning was frigid, yesterday's storm leaving its icy mark. The lights in the house were out, but the sunlight streaming through made up for it.

I inhaled the cinnamon-scented steam rising off the top of the cup with a sigh. What a blissful way to start the day.

"The who of the what now?"

Ugh. Right. I was so caught up in enjoying the moment, I had forgotten I wasn't alone. Taking a long, much needed sip, I peeled my eyes from the empty space on the wall and looked at Stella. "The Sisters of the River," I answered.

"As in..."

"The River Styx." I shivered, suddenly feeling the chill of the day in my very bones. When Stella manifested this morning, she acted as though yesterday didn't happen and I had no choice but to play along. There was no arguing with the ghost once she had her mind made up. Instead, I chose to fill her in on the article Joe dug up online. "Apparently, it was some big cult back in the day. At least that's what the academic wrote in his paper. It was all very foofoo."

My familiar's eyes darted to the couch where Harry Houdini lay sprawled on his back, snoring. "More foofoo than that?"

I chuckled.

"I guess not. Anyway, the thesis was a bit out there, but some of the points struck a chord," I explained. "According to the guy's research, The Sisters of the River had quite the following."

"As cults often do."

Nodding, I sipped on the latte and continued. "We're talking people all over the world, all women."

"Why only women?" Stella asked.

"That's what I wanted to know too," I agreed. "Think about it. A group dedicated to the worship of a specific deity, secretive behavior, and they're all women?"

Eyebrows slanting, Stella's mouth gaped as she said, "You think they were a coven."

"I do. I'm guessing Joe does too, since he forwarded the article."

Stella zeroed in on the bowl of sugar cubes left on the counter. Her body gained some solidness as she reached for a cube, gripping it with ghostly fingers. In one smooth motion, Stella tossed the sugar in the air, opening her mouth to catch it. I cringed as it dropped through her body and hit the floor with a low thud.

"Trying new tricks?"

Stella shrugged. "So, what happened to these witches?"

"That's the thing," I answered. "They basically vanished off the face of the earth. At some point in the nineties, any mention of the sisters disappeared. It was as though they were erased from existence. No one has heard of them since."

The ghost rubbed her chin slowly, eyes never leaving the bowl of sugar. What was her obsession with the damn thing? "Strange," she whispered. "Do you think they disbanded their Devil-worshipping circus?"

"I don't know. According to the thesis, the cult likely lost steam as members dropped away." My eyes met Stella's heated gaze. "Though that seems unlikely, doesn't it? A coven wouldn't abandon its deity, nor would they stop their practice."

"Unless something made them stop."

I considered her words. What could happen to make an entire coven disappear? It didn't make any sense. Most witches practiced in groups and a deity as specific as Hades—assuming that was who they worshipped, as their name implied—would not be abandoned so freely. Unless...

"What if they didn't stop practicing?" I mused. "What if they're still around? Hiding."

Silence hung over the room. I looked at Stella to gauge her reaction, but the ghost was buffering again. A second later, she was gone. Eyes rolling to the back of my head, I started for the living room to get Harry's butt off the couch when I heard my name being called.

Whipping to face my familiar, I choked on whatever was lodged in my throat as I took in her worried expression. "What's wrong?"

"I'm not sure," Stella said. "One minute I was here, the next I was back there again."

"There?"

Stella grimaced. "The woods. Where they found me. I can't explain it, but it was like I had to return. Don't ask me what for because I couldn't tell you."

Wetting my cracked lips, I put my hands on my

hips and let out a slow breath. Stella's strange freezes have become much more frequent and frankly, were freaking me the heck out. And what did she mean by having to go back to the hiking trails? It sounded straight out of a horror movie. Though she seemed very distraught about it. I pressed my tongue to the roof of my mouth, an idea rolling around in my head.

If I couldn't talk to Arthur Rutherford without pissing the ghost off, perhaps I could find a reason for the sheriff to reopen the case. Then he'd have an excuse to question Stella's husband and my hands would be washed clean of the task.

"You might be on the right track," I told Stella. "Tell you what, I'll go over there on my way into town and check it out. Want to come with?"

The look Stella gave me told me she most definitely did not. I couldn't blame her. If I was walking around all dead, the last place I'd want to be was the scene of where I bit it. And I saw how shaken she was when she got transported to the trails.

"Actually," I said quickly, "I can go alone. No point dragging both of us over there if it's a dead end. No pun intended."

Stella did not appear convinced. She gave me a once over and pouted her fake lips. "Can you ask the bloodsucker to join? You're not exactly the hiking type," she said. Then, glancing at my shirt and jeans added, "And how about putting on clothes from this century?"

Good to know the situation hadn't altered her personality. I brushed her off and was about to argue, then paused. While I wasn't about to call Joe to come to my rescue simply because Stella didn't think I couldn't handle a hiking trail, I wasn't dumb. The woods were not the safest place for someone as inexperienced as me. Not that I'd ever let Stella know this, but I was a bit worried about going there alone. The area had no phone reception; if something happened, I'd have no way to call for help.

Casting one last glance at the abundantly relaxed raccoon on my couch, I picked up my phone and typed a message, heading for the door.

"Did you call the vampire?" Stella asked.

I deadpanned from the open doorway. "Better. I called a witch."

CHAPTER 7

Fifteen minutes after leaving the house, I was leaning against the side of the Beetle in one of the few parking lots leading to the hiking trails. The massive trees around me cast dreadful shadows on the gravel road cutting through the forest, painting less than a serene picture of the Orchard Hollow woods. I had no idea why so many people enjoyed coming here. To me, the forest presented itself as a gloomy danger zone full of unknown creatures. A mosquito buzzed next to my ear, and I swatted it away maniacally. Ew. Gross.

In the distance, a car's engine neared, and I straightened out, watching the road. A few seconds later, a red mustang peeked out from behind the dense foliage. I waited patiently, my smile broadening as Cilia parked and climbed out of the car. She wore an all black turtleneck sweater with dark blue leggings that seemed to be insulated for the cold weather. A sporty pack with a water bottle strapped to its side hung over her shoulder, and she had on very sensible hiking boots that went up past her ankles.

I looked down at my vintage leather loafers and frowned. How I hated it when Stella was right; I was not at all prepared for this.

"Hey, Addison," Cilia said as she approached. "Want to tell me why we're here?"

Right. I forgot that I didn't explain anything to the witch when I called her, basically begging her to join me. It actually surprised me Cilia even showed up, considering I probably sounded like a vague lunatic. Say what you will, but I was pretty certain telling someone the ghost of a dead woman talked to you was a task best done in person.

I gathered whatever courage I could and channeled my inner Stella. "So, here's the thing..." I said. "I kind of, sort of have an unusual familiar."

"You mean like a cat?" Cilia asked.

"I mean like a ghost."

It took all of two seconds for Cilia's eyes to bulge out of their sockets, and she caught herself as a chuckle burst from her lips. "Why am I not surprised, Addison?" she asked. "You can never half-ass anything."

While Cilia's wicked grin spread, I tried to gauge her reaction. "You don't think it's weird that a dead woman is my magical sidekick?"

"Oh, it's weird as hell," the witch agreed. "But also very on brand for you. I like it. Tell me you didn't call me all the way out here for that."

Gnawing on my bottom lip, I checked the very empty parking lot and scowled. A part of me wished there were tourists here today so I could run away and not involve Cilia in mine and Stella's bizarro plans. But we were already here, and I knew Cilia would be helpful. She was a competent witch and had a grasp on her magic in a way I didn't. I had the distinct feeling we would need magic if we were to uncover anything the cops might have missed all those years ago.

"Long story short," I started to explain, choosing my words wisely. "The ghost of a woman named Stella Rutherford is tied to me for the rest of time and she has somewhat of a situation on her hands. Stella doesn't remember anything about her death except that it was not an accident as the police deemed it to be. Considering my last two—let's say notable—police encounters, she asked me to help. And I asked you to come here so we can see what we can sleuth out. This was where...it happened."

Cilia twirled around, her one eyebrow quirking. "What? Right here?"

"No, of course not," I answered. "On the trails. Bottom of a cliff."

"Could she have tripped and fallen over?"

I frowned. "That's what the police thought. Or some of them. The sheriff doesn't believe it, but his hands are tied. Don't ask why."

"You don't agree with them?"

"Not at all," I said confidently.

Suddenly, Cilia's lips formed an O, and she sucked in a sharp breath. "Wait, did you say Rutherford? As in Arthur Rutherford?"

I nodded.

"I think I remember this! Happened a while back, right?"

My gaze locked on hers. "Do you know Stella's husband?"

"Goddess, no," Cilia scoffed. "We're not from the same side of the tracks. It was in the paper, though. His wife's death. I remember reading about it. And she's your familiar? Small world."

That's one way of looking at it. Annoying world is another.

I crammed my cold hands into my jacket pocket

and tipped my chin toward the entrance to the trails. "What do you say? Want to help me solve a murder?"

"A possible murder," Cilia corrected. "And hell yes!"

As we crossed the road and made our way into the dense foliage, my body grew rigid. I could feel the energy of the ley lines that ran under the woods with each step. Here in the deep of the forest, the pull of their magic was so much stronger and I wondered if maybe the place where Stella died had anything to do with our connection. Perhaps the magic of the ley lines tied her to me. Another thought briefly entered my mind, and I tried my hardest to stifle it down. *What if solving Stella's case breaks our bond?*

I was so not ready to deal with that can of worms.

A twig snapped in the distance and I grabbed Cilia's wrist, squeezing the living daylights out of it.

"Probably a warlock replenishing," Cilia said assuredly.

I let go of her, cheeks burning with embarrassment. She was right, of course. Warlocks often came out to these woods to be closer to the ley lines, as they needed the energy to replenish their magic. Unlike witches who pull directly from the elements found on earth, warlocks used their own energy to cast. Which meant that every spell cost them. Tapping into the ley lines gave warlocks a boost of sorts and prevented them from fizzling out. It was a pain in the butt, I was certain. It was also the reason the warlocks held an unspoken grudge against witches like a bunch of spoiled children.

Moody little bastards.

Another loud snap broke me from my daydreaming and I stopped stock-still. Before me, Cilia held onto a nearby branch while one of her boots hung in mid-air. I rushed toward her, grabbing her by the shoulder and dragging her to me and away from the drop-off she stumbled into. Her breath quickened, then relaxed as she found solid ground again.

"Thanks," she whispered. "Close call."

We inched toward the edge and looked down. Saliva pooled in my mouth and I took one big swallow as my gaze floated down. And down. And down. All the way to the bottom of what appeared to be a pretty hefty cliff.

I looked at the map on my phone. "I think this is it."

"Convenient. We didn't even have to walk far."

As my breath evened out, I scanned the area, eyes cutting through the trees and the makeshift passage we walked to get here. It was pretty convenient, wasn't it? The cliff Stella was found at the bottom of was located in an interesting part of the woods. Close enough to the main road that it didn't take long for someone to get here, yet hidden enough that no one would stumble across it easily. I looked down into the horrifying abyss that spelled Stella's final moments.

"Does this look like a normal hiking location to you?" I asked.

Cilia shook her head vigorously. "The slope of the trail combined with the overgrowth on our way here tells me people don't venture out here often."

I gaped at her, slack-jawed.

"What?" Cilia threw her hands up and shrugged. "My family was outdoorsy."

I laughed. "From your outdoorsy experience, do you think someone like Stella Rutherford would use this part of the trails for recreational purposes? And is it me or does this place give you the heebie-jeebies?"

Beside me, Cilia's feet shuffled as she turned to inspect the tree-lined path we stood on. Her arm stretched out, and she pulled a leaf from a nearby bush, sniffing it like a search dog at the airport. Her brow creased deeply. "I don't know about tourists, but I can tell you that no witch or warlock would come here." She shoved the leaf in my face and wiggled it around. "Belladonna."

Yikes. I looked around, spotting similar foliage all over the place. Despite growing up with a Gran who had the green thumb of all green thumbs, I didn't inherit the ability to use herbs in my magic. Granted,

I didn't inherit much of my family's magic at all, at least not the witch kind. Still, even I knew that any place with this much Belladonna was to be avoided like the plague. The dumb plant was basically a magical kryptonite. Its potent energy killed most spells and potions simply by being near them. I wasn't sure what that meant for Stella's situation, but at least we knew there was little chance a paranormal was involved. At least not in the magical sense.

My stomach lurched as another thought occurred to me. "There goes my plan to try a locator spell."

"Hmm, true," Cilia mused. "What were you hoping to locate?"

"I honestly have no clue. Something to lead us in the right direction, I guess."

Peeling her gaze from mine, Cilia slung her bag around and dug inside. Her arm disappeared into the leather and she continued to search, a frustrated look flashing across her face. Her hand was buried so deep inside, I thought she might pull out a rabbit. "Got it!" Cilia yelped, whipping out a metal contraption.

She twisted it around and around and in seconds, a long metal arm formed in her grasp. At the end of it, a metal disk sparkled as the light streaming in between the trees hit it.

"What is that?" I asked.

The witch smirked. "The next best thing to a dowsing rod. Metal detector."

"Is there anything you *don't* have in that bag?" I pouted my lips. "Got any snacks in there?"

Cilia rolled her eyes and lowered the metal detector to the ground. Her free hand reached back into the bag and she pulled out an energy bar, tossing it my way. The bar hit me square in the jaw, falling lamely at my feet. I had half the mind to leave it, but the insistence of my growling belly forced me to swallow my pride. Scarfing it down, I turned my attention back to Cilia. "You really think this thing will work?"

"Only one way to find out," the witch answered.

With a flick of a button, the contraption whirred to life, and she began scanning the ground for anything out of the ordinary. The area nearest the cliff came back empty and Cilia soon moved further into the trees, continuing to run the machine over the earth as she walked. The buzzing sound that followed her movements started to fade, and I had to strain my eyes to see her in the shadow of the tree trunks.

Checking the time, I scowled when I realized I was running way behind to meet Joe as I promised.

About to call Cilia back, I opened my mouth right as she yelled out, "Over here!"

My heart jolted. Feet moving quickly, I cut

through the trees and ran toward the direction of her voice. A few large oak trees over, Cilia stood with the metal detector screeching in her hands.

She pointed to the base of one tree. "There."

Dropping to my knees, I shoved my fingers into the dirt and started to dig. Pieces of the ground stuck under my nails and I cringed at the gross wetness that sloshed around beneath my palms. At my back, Cilia's bag rustled and a moment later, a metal hand trowel landed next to me. I looked up at Cilia, grinning. "You really are prepared for anything."

"Never leave the house without a minimum of five emergency items."

"Noted," I said, returning to the hole I was digging. I tried not think about what emergency might require my new friend to use a tiny shovel.

Ten excruciating minutes later, and my arm felt like it might fall off. The trowel Cilia provided helped, but I was way out of shape and by no means prepared to dig a small grave in the forest. Another minute more and I might have given up. Or collapsed from exhaustion.

My arm tensed and I gave the trowel another push, the metal clicking against an object in the ground.

I stopped breathing.

"What is that?" Cilia asked.

Ignoring her, I used the pointy end of the trowel to spread the dirt, a hot lump forming in my throat as something glistened in the hole. Shaking fingers reaching in, I pulled out the loot we found and held it up for Cilia.

"Is that a—"

"Tennis bracelet," I said.

Tossing the trowel away, I got up and inspected the bracelet. It was on the smaller size, made for a thinner wrist. Instead of the usual diamonds, this bracelet was made entirely of pearls, and I could feel the weight of them in my palm. I took out my phone and turned on the flashlight, shining it over the bracelet. "The clasp is broken," I told Cilia.

She snatched the bracelet from my hands and brought it up to her face. Turning it around, Cilia checked the broken clasp, nodding. "I think this might have belonged to your friend."

"Why do you say that?"

Cilia pointed to the clasp and the small initial carved into the gold. S. As in Stella.

It was a stretch, but what were the chances that we would find a bracelet in the woods not far from where Stella died? And why was it buried?

I was about to ask Cilia what she thought when the witch beat me to it.

"Look at that," she instructed, pointing.

As I did, my heart sank to my feet. The three pearls nearest the clasp were a different color than the rest—darker and dreadful. I swallowed the bile rolling into my throat and blinked away the burning tears that welled behind my lids. "Is that blood?"

Cilia nodded.

Peeling my eyes from the bracelet, I glanced past her shoulder toward the path leading to the cliff. Stella's bracelet was not here by accident. Someone buried it under the tree, someone who wanted to get rid of it. I was pretty sure the blood on the damn thing had a lot to do with that decision.

While I had very little idea of what happened to my friend out here, one thing was glaringly certain. Stella was right to think she didn't die of natural causes. That blood was hers—I just knew it.

My head pounded as I realized another important fact.

The tennis bracelet wasn't cheap. Except for the blood stains, the pearls appeared to be in pristine condition and the gold clasp looked intricately designed, like it was crafted by a master jeweler. Even I could tell the difference between costume jewelry and a piece this impressive. The initial on it gave me pause. People didn't often stamp their own jewelry. Unless it was a gift, one that I could easily picture Stella loving.

I blinked rapidly, taking it all in.

There was only one person I could think of in my familiar's life who might have given her the bracelet.

I sighed. I finally had a clue, and yet I felt absolutely gutted. My ghostly best friend was not going to like this one bit. I could only imagine what she would do once she realized I went behind her back to grill her husband.

Get ready for the tantrum of a lifetime, I told myself. I only hoped the farmhouse would survive Stella's wrath.

CHAPTER 8

There were no words to describe how much I hated canceling on Joe, but after the discovery of the bracelet, which now burned a hole in my pocket, I couldn't sit around looking at old dusty books and searching for a cult that might not exist. Stella's death and afterlife were on the line.

Should I have handed in the bracelet to the sheriff? Probably. Did I trust him to do the right thing and reopen the case of Stella's possible murder? Also probably.

Then how did the stupid trinket find its way into a ziplock bag and then into my pocket?

If Stella were here, she'd have told me I did the right thing following my gut. I knew the police would muck up the case even further given the chance, and I did plan on handing over the evidence I technically sort of kind of stole. Except Stella wasn't here and if she were, she'd likely try to run the car off the road since I was literally on my way to prove her husband killed her.

I made for one shady friend.

The Rutherfords lived so far out of town that even my GPS started to get confused as I drove the winding seaside road. By the tenth time it asked me to confirm the address, I had to turn the annoying thing off. Besides, there wasn't much out this way and, by the way Stella described her lavish house, I knew I couldn't miss it.

With the cliffs on my right and the water on my left, the drive was a serene experience. If it weren't for where I was headed, I might have come here again.

The road swerved to the left, and a tunnel came into view ahead of me. I never liked driving through them. The deep darkness made me feel it would never end. Like I was entering a doorway that would take me away for good. The rational part of me knew I was letting my imagination get the better of me, but it didn't stop my magic from lighting up my fingers.

After another fifteen minutes of driving, two energy drinks, and a gas station sandwich that wasn't as fresh as it should have been, I was starting to feel antsy and couldn't wait to get out of the car. Luckily, or unluckily, depending on how you looked at it, I didn't need to wait much longer. Turning off the main road onto what I could only describe as a driveway set for heaven, I tried not to drool as I drove up the entrance to the Rutherford estate. Large oak trees crowded the length of the driveway and the smell of the sea being lingered in the air as I wove down the path to the main house.

Mansion was probably a better word for it.

For anyone approaching, there was only one thing the mansion spelled out: the people inside had money. I mean, the fountain marking the turnabout before the entrance was a dead giveaway.

I looked around as I pulled up, trying to find somewhere to leave the Beetle. When it became apparent that there were no spots available, I opted to leave the car on the driveway and walk over.

Those five minutes were the longest of my entire life. Each step was a reminder of the riff I was about to put between myself and my familiar, a riff so big she may never speak to me again.

The house grew taller before me as I neared. I

shook my head and rolled my shoulders, feet planted firmly on the stoop of the front door. Reaching a rubbery finger for the doorbell, I told myself there was no turning back now and pushed.

A Mariachi tune broke the silence of the front yard and I frowned. There was no way Stella would let something so tacky exist in her house. I briefly wondered who was responsible for the awful doorbell selection, but as it turned out, I had little time to dwell on the enthralling mystery. The large doors swung open, revealing a small man in a crisp white suit.

"Rutherford residence. How may I help you?" the man asked.

"Hello. I-I..." Pausing to collect myself, I tried again. "I'm here to see Arthur Rutherford." Then, channeling my inner Stella, added, "It's rather urgent, if you don't mind."

It turned out the man did mind. "Do you have an appointment?"

"Trust me, Mr. Rutherford will want to hear what I have to say."

Clearing his throat, the man looked me up and down, his face revealing nothing. "Yes, well, I'm afraid whether that is true or not is irrelevant. One must have an appointment to speak to Mr. Rutherford. He is rather indisposed at the moment."

Indisposed because he's killing another wife? My cheeks burnt as I tried to think of a way to get the protector of the door on my side. What was it that Gran said? More bees with the truth.

Recovering quickly, I found my truth and went straight for the jugular.

"You can tell Mr. Rutherford that I was friends with his wife," I said, "and that I have information about her death he might find interesting."

On cue, the man's face blanched, and he cleared his throat again, then held up an index finger in my impatient face. "One moment please."

When the guardian of the door departed, I popped my head through the open doorway and looked around. My jaw hit the floor as I took in the large foyer that stretched the entire length of the majestic home. Even from here, I could see large windows encasing the rear of the house showing off glimpses of the football field-sized backyard. There were hints of a sprawling garden somewhere in the distance, but what I couldn't take my eyes off was the pool. It was likely the size of the entire farmhouse.

My eyes left the yard and traveled up the two-story ceilings of the foyer. At the turret-framed top, three gargantuan chandeliers hung down, the lights on despite it being the early morning. On either side of the hall, closed doors piqued my curiosity, and I battled the urge to burst into one of them.

Footsteps sounded from behind a door, and I quickly shoved myself through the doorway and to the front stoop. The steps got closer. My heart pitter-pattered in my chest and I could hear it thunder in my ears. It was so loud I couldn't hear myself think.

The door creaked, opening wider. I anchored my feet down, forcing myself to stand stone-still. A second later, a silver fox appeared before me. His eyes were crinkled at the edges and his brow was creased slightly, much too little for someone of his age. For an early Tuesday morning, the man was sure dressed to the nines. He wore a suit that made him look like he was on his way to a gala, not lounging at home.

I recognized him instantly.

"Hello, Mr. Rutherford," I said politely. "My name is Piper Addison."

"You're here to speak to me about what happened to Stella?"

My stomach pitched violently. I was not ready for this at all. "I am," I answered. "Is there somewhere more private we can speak? It's just that what I have to say... I'm not sure you want other people hearing it."

For some reason, the statement earned me a grin that revealed the world's greatest set of teeth. "Believe me, miss, the front door is as private as you'll get in this house." He glanced over his shoulder. "Too many prying eyes watching and ears listening, you understand?"

I certainly did not understand, but returned his smile, anyway. "Yes, well, I don't know how to say this, but I'm looking into your wife's death."

"Oh," Arthur said, "I didn't realize you were with the police."

"I'm not," I clarified. "I am—was—a friend of your wife's."

"I see. Funny. She never mentioned you."

I bit down on my tongue. Hard. My web of lies was starting to come apart even before I asked what I came here to ask. Wracking my fuzzy brain for an excuse, I said, "We didn't see each other that often. You know how some people are: you don't need to see them a lot for them to know you care."

Arthur looked down at his designer loafers, then back at me again.

"Of course," he said. "May I ask why you decided to look into Stella's death? After all this time."

That is a great question. Quick, Piper. Think of an excuse that doesn't make it sound like you're a serial killer. Definitely don't talk about the ghost.

"I thought I told you not to come here."

My heart jolted as Stella's voice rang in my ear. I forced out the meek giggle Arthur's way and turned my head slightly to see said ghost leaning against the side of the mansion. Her eyes shot daggers at me and while she didn't say anything, I read the message loud and clear. My clothes are going to pay for this later.

Collecting myself, I faced Stella's husband, saying, "Everything about the way Stella died didn't seem like an accident to me. It never did," I explained. "I lost my grandmother not that long ago, and after, things changed. I guess you could say I changed."

"Turned into a bit of an amateur sleuth, did you?" Arthur chuckled.

"You could say that. In this case, though, my changing might work in both our favors."

That's it. Lay it on thick. Get him on your side, then get him to talk.

A cold breeze ruffled my hair as Stella waved her hand in front of my face. "Oh, darling, that won't work with Arthur. He can smell false compliments from a mile away," she said, annoyingly. I shook my hand and hoped she got the clue and stayed quiet. She didn't. "Why don't you come out and say it? Tell him I'm right here. And make sure you don't forget to say that I don't agree with anything you're doing. Also, while you're at it, tell the man I miss him."

Closing my eyes tightly, I wished her away. When

I opened them again, Stella was still there, and her husband looked like he was one word away from calling the cops. I sighed, rolling my shoulders to stand up straighter. "I'll cut right to the chase," I said. "Whatever reason, I had to open the can of worms that was your wife's untimely death is not the point. The point is that evidence has come to light since I started doing whatever it is I'm doing."

I reached into my pocket and pulled out the ziplock bag. Stretching out my arm, I presented it to Arthur like a game show host, twirling the bag around so he can see the pearl tennis bracelet inside.

"What do you have there?" Arthur asked, reaching for the bracelet.

I yanked it back, refusing to part with the only piece of the puzzle I had.

Beside me, Stella poked her nose over my shoulder to inspect my loot. "What is that gaudy thing?" she asked.

My face blanched. I clenched my teeth together.

"It's your tennis bracelet," I said out of the side of my mouth.

Stella's hand pressed to her heart in mock shock, a disgusted look on her face. "Why, darling, I would never wear pearls."

Paying her little mind, I looked at Arthur. "Are you telling me you've never seen this before?"

"I have not," he answered.

"You didn't buy this for Stella? You didn't have her name initialed on the clasp?"

Mirroring his dead wife, Arthur locked his eyes on mine, saying, "It's made of pearls."

What the heck is wrong with these people? As far as I could tell, the bracelet was stunning, expensive. And it had Stella's initial on it. I buried my outrage deep down and tried to appear less annoyed with the old man. "I don't know what you have against the bracelet, but this belonged to your wife. I'm sure of it. So, if you are absolutely convinced you didn't buy it, perhaps she purchased it herself."

Taking one long, pensive look at the bag in my hands, Arthur rubbed the bridge of his nose, seemingly over my presence at his front door. He glanced over his shoulder at the door, then around the driveway. If I didn't know we were here alone, I'd have thought he was signaling a sniper to take my nosy butt out.

"My wife would never wear that," he finally uttered. "If you'd like, I'd be more than happy to show you her jewelry collection. I can guarantee you will not find a pearl in sight. Stella was partial to all things ruby and diamond. What you have in your hand may as well be costume jewelry, as far as I'm concerned."

I knew I came here to get the man to confess to Stella's murder, but I wasn't so sure anymore. What if

I got it wrong, and this bracelet wasn't my familiar's at all? What if I made a mistake?

I was about to tuck my tail between my legs and run out of there when Arthur said, "Actually, now that I think about it, that thing looks like Nicki might wear it."

"Ugh, she would." Stella groaned.

My head was spinning from how hard it was to keep up with these two.

"Who was are you talking about? And who's Nicki?"

"My daughter," Arthur said at the same time as Stella whispered, "the Wicked Witch of the West."

I filed the comment away for later inspection and chose to focus all my attention on her husband. Pinning Arthur with a serious glare, I asked, "Is your daughter home? I'd love to ask her about the bracelet in person."

"She's not. Nicki is away for the week. You're welcome to come by when she returns, though I doubt you'd get much out of her."

My eyes thinned into narrow lines. "And why is that?" I asked.

"Nicki and my wife didn't get along." When my face scrunched up, Arthur held his hands up defensively. "I know how it sounds. Stepmother and step-daughter fighting. It's a tale as old as time. Not for a lack of trying on Stella's part, too. I love my daughter, but even I must admit she's prickly at times."

Prickly enough to kill? I wondered. I had to stop myself from jumping to conclusions, even though I could see the wheels turning in Stella's head beside me. My familiar was thinking the same thing.

"Will that be all?" Arthur asked, checking his thick gold watch. "I really must get the day started."

I smiled, but it didn't reach my eyes. The entire exchange left me confused and disappointed all at once. I was so certain of Arthur's guilt on the way here, I never stopped to think about what it might mean if I was wrong. And to think the bracelet wasn't even Stella's. What a joke.

Thanking Arthur for his time, I promised to return when his daughter was home and made the dreadful walk back to the Beetle. This time, I wasn't walking alone.

"I can't believe you came here after I specifically told you not to."

I spun around toward Stella's pretentious face. "I don't really care what you specifically told me to do," I told my familiar. "I am not your employee. I am your friend, and I am trying to find out who freaking killed you."

In all our time together, I had gotten quite used to Stella's outbursts, but never had they been so viciously directed at me. Sure, she enjoyed teasing me about my outfits, my hair, my pathetic love life. But this was something else entirely. It was as though Stella was purposefully getting in the way of me figuring out how she died. As though she didn't want to know. My eyes rounded as I stopped in dead in my tracks. "Do you not want me to help you?"

"I'm not sure anymore," Stella said solemnly.

Anger bubbled up within me. I didn't know why I was so mad at my familiar. She wasn't sure anymore? What did that mean? Stella came to me, finally opening up about her feelings and now she was yanking them all back. I felt tricked and used and... well, I didn't know what else. Somewhere deep down I knew there was a chance that solving Stella's death might break our bond and help her cross over. Which, if I cared to admit it, would really suck. But the part of me that cared for the stubborn ghost knew that it would help her. It would give her closure. Why would she ask me for help to do so, then change her mind? What kind of—

"Watch out!"

Stella's panicked voice snapped me back to reality. My eyes bulged as I took in the massive magical rip in the air inches in front of me. I gasped, tripping over my feet and falling forward face-first into the void. Frigid fingers gripped my arm and pulled me back. I yelled out as a searing pain shot through my body. My arm felt like it had been pulled out of its socket. Head spinning around, I looked at the rip that closed and vanished before my eyes as though it never existed. Breath coming short, I twisted my neck to gaze at Stella Rutherford. "Did you—"

"Save your life?" she asked. "I did. And you're welcome."

"T-thank you. What was that?"

"Looked like the same thing that happened in your bedroom."

"But bigger," I whispered, shivering from the cold of Stella's ghostly touch that lingered on my skin. I turned my arm around, surprised it was in one piece. The pain from my familiar's surprising strength started to recede, and I was relieved that no bones broke during her heroic act of saving my sorry behind.

We stood in the lavish driveway of the Rutherford estate, a few feet from the Beetle. Silence enveloped us and for some reason, I couldn't will my legs to move. When I finally regained my composure and climbed into the car, I didn't start it, choosing instead to stare out the window blankly. A million thoughts ran through my head, but only one stood out front and center.

Whatever my magic was up to, it was getting worse. I needed to get a hold of it. I briefly recalled Joe and the Sisters of the River. Deep down, I felt that finding out more about those witches would aid my current situation. And if I were lucky, it might help me understand who I was and what the heck was happening to me.

CHAPTER 9

"**I**f you really want to talk to the little devil, you should get her out of the house," Stella suggested while I downed the last of my dinner margaritas.

After spending the remainder of the day out of it and thinking only about what happened at the Rutherford estate, I needed to wind down. I barely remembered driving home, let alone making the pasta that now sat half-eaten before me. What I did vividly recall was that absolutely bizarre rip in the air and how I would have bitten the bullet if it wasn't for Stella Rutherford pulling me out.

I also remembered her husband pretty much pointing the finger at his own daughter.

Carefully, I eyed Stella from behind the murky glass trying to read her expression with no luck. At first, I thought she was glad Nicki ended up on my suspect list, but now I wasn't so convinced. Licking the salt off the rim, I asked, "And how do you propose I do that? Invite her out to dinner?"

"In a way," my familiar answered. "For as long as I've known Nicki, she had a standing date with herself at the Coral Reef."

My heart pitter-pattered as I sat the glass down, my interest peaking. Why did the daughter of a millionaire enjoy *that* place?

The Coral Reef restaurant was fine by most people's standards, mine especially, but I couldn't picture Arthur's daughter there. Not unless she enjoyed smelling like burnt fries for the rest of the week.

Stella shrugged. "I have no idea, but she loves it. Calls it her home away from home, whatever that means. Nicki was odd like that."

I tried not to take offense at the fact that Stella's definition of weird was dining with the likes of me.

"When is she usually there?" I asked.

The ghost's eyes landed on an invisible watch on her wrist. "She should be at the restaurant for the next hour or so."

"Geez, Stella! A little warning next time. I'm literally in my pajamas." I looked down the length of myself and groaned at the marinara stain across my thigh and the alcohol on my breath. "I can't drive right now."

"Brush your hair and call a cab. Not like you need a ball gown for that place."

She had me there. The beauty of the Coral Reef was that you could show up in your underwear and get service.

Following Stella's advice, I ran a comb through my messy hair, braided it loosely, and put on a pair of worn-out denim leggings. Twenty minutes later and the cab I called was pulling up to the packed parking lot in front of the restaurant. I cringed at the flickering neon sign over the building depicting a hot dog and fries holding hands. The name Coral Reef, spelled out in cursive letters beneath them had seen better days. The paint chipping so deeply, I worried pieces of it might drop right on my head as I walked past. I thanked the driver and climbed out, my legs slowing the closer I got to the entrance. Speaking to Arthur at his home was one thing, but stalking Stella's stepdaughter was quite another. Maybe Joe was right, and I really did have trouble drawing the line. One of these days, it was going to get me into trouble. I straightened my shoulders and sighed. *Here's hoping today was not that day.*

For a weekday evening, the restaurant was surprisingly busy. There were sounds of plates clinking in the kitchen, and the loud voices of patrons filled the air. I tried to find an empty booth amidst the worn-out leather and wood tabletops, quickly remembering I wasn't here to dine alone.

"Be right with you," a cheerful voice cried out.

I turned to watch the evening shift server balance four plates and a pot of coffee as she sauntered into the kitchen. The open layout of the cooking area was a bold choice, considering the state of the kitchen wasn't faring much better than the remainder of the place. I caught the start of a grease fire and quickly looked away, nauseous.

While I waited for the server to come back, I scanned the people eating. There was a family nearest to me with three kids, all of whom were in the middle of what appeared to be a food fight starting. The booth table off the back housed several teenagers laughing wildly and clinking their glasses of pop. A few more groups filled the tight space, but for the most part, the Coral Reef was occupied by singles like myself. My eyes narrowed on the one girl that matched Nicki's description. Shockingly, she didn't seem too out of place. Her long dark hair was half tied in a loose ponytail and she wore a pair of brown overalls that made her look more like she was an artist at the local college and not a millionaire's daughter. Her eyes concentrated on the book before her and she bit the bottom of her lip as she read, taking occasional sips of coffee.

"Table for one?" the server asked over my shoulder.

I jolted, peeling my eyes away from Nicki. "I'm actually meeting someone. I think I see her, but thank you."

"No problem, hun. I'll be by in a few to take your order."

I really hoped she wouldn't.

My courage dissipating, I walked toward Nicki's table, my imaginary tail ducking between my legs. When I reached her, I got the distinct urge to turn around and run away. Pushing all my weight onto my heels to keep myself from moving, I eyed Nicki. She didn't notice me hovering over her table, being completely engulfed in her reading. I harrumphed, begging for her attention. When she looked up, she did not appear pleased.

"I already placed my order," she said.

"Oh, I don't work here." *Do I look like I work here?* I double checked my outfit to make sure it didn't resemble that of the server. "I'm actually looking for you. My name is Piper. Piper Addison. I was a friend of Stella Rutherford's and was hoping to ask you a couple of questions, if you don't mind."

Nicki quirked a bushy eyebrow, and I added, "Your dad said I could find you here."

The lie rolled off my tongue so smoothly. I hated that it didn't bother me at all. Since when was I a professional liar?

Nicki's mouth opened and closed like she was trying to think of a way to get out of the conversation. With an annoyed sigh, she closed the tome she was reading and gestured to the empty chair across from her. "I don't have a lot of time, but I can answer a couple questions, I suppose."

"Thank you," I said as I slid into the chair. It scraped across the old linoleum, the sound loud enough to raise the undead.

"How did you know Stella?" Nicki asked before I could speak.

I widened my fake smile. "We were friends from back in the day. She spoke very highly of you."

"Ha!" Nicki guffawed. "Are you sure we're talking about the same Stella? Because the one I knew couldn't stand my guts."

Hmm. I thought it was the other way around. I briefly wondered how much of the relationship between my familiar and her stepdaughter could have been mended by better communication. Tucking my wayward thoughts away, I turned my focus back to Nicki. "Same Stella, I'm afraid," I said.

"I'm trying to find out what happened to her the day she died."

Nicki's face dropped before my eyes and her pupils dilated. Her long, slender fingers worked at a loose cuticle until a spot of blood appeared on her thumb. She swallowed hard, taking another sip of stale coffee before speaking. "She fell off a cliff. What's there to find out?"

"The circumstances of her death don't align with her behavioral patterns."

Honestly, who are you even? Behavioral patterns? I really needed to stop bingeing those late-night cop shows. Hoping Nicki didn't chalk me up to be some lunatic, I placed my hands on the table and leaned in slightly. "Do you remember anything out of the usual happening the day she went into the woods? Did she seem out of sorts that morning?"

"Stella was always out of sorts," Nicki rebutted. "But no, nothing like that."

Her eyes got even wider until she resembled a cartoon deer. She also resembled someone who was lying, a trait I had come to recognize quite easily in the last few months. On account of all the murderers I was chasing like a complete weirdo. I pulled my hands away, crossing my arms over my chest. "What is it you're not telling me?"

Nicki's cheeks turned bright red.

"I'm not with the police, if that's what you're worried about," I whispered.

This seemed to snap her out of her daze. Her chin tipped up, and she stared at me defiantly, her brown eyes searing into mine. "You should consider that a blessing," she bit out. "Lot of good those morons did last time around."

"I take it you didn't agree with how the local police department handled the case?"

"Are you kidding?" Nicki exclaimed, her palms slapping the table. "Those idiots botched it up so bad, there was no way anyone could figure out what really happened to Stella."

For a second, a flash of emotion akin to sadness covered Nicki's face. Was it all an act? Did the kid actually like my dead familiar? I didn't have a chance to read her expression longer because Nicki leaned in, her face so close to mine I could smell the lavender perfume she wore. "Look, I'm going to tell you something, but it doesn't leave this table. Got it?"

I nodded.

Satisfied with my answer, Nicki leaned back, her shoulders relaxing. Mine followed suit immediately.

"Back when Stella was...here, we got into it. A lot," she explained.

Don't I know it.

"Anyway, I was dead-set on dad leaving her to the

point that I hired a PI. I figured if I could get some dirt on her, I could break them up." Nicki's lips twitched. "Stella didn't come from the best place, so I thought the same as everyone else, that she was only with my dad for his money."

I frowned. "Stella loved your father."

"I know that now," Nicki answered. "But back then, I wanted her gone."

"Did the PI find anything?"

Hesitation clouded her features and for a moment, I thought Nicki would clam up and ask me to leave. Instead, she rubbed her temples and looked at her coffee cup, pushing it away instead of drinking. "He found something all right," she said, her voice lower. "It turned out Stella had a whole other life before she met my dad. She was engaged to some guy. Sam. Collins, I think. They were together for a real long time and then Stella up and ended it. The investigator said he believed she met my father and called the engagement off."

"That doesn't seem so strange," I countered. "People break engagements off all the time."

In front of me, Nicki's posture tensed. "How many of those people get a restraining order against their exes?"

Come again? My head did a double-take, and I gulped the excess saliva pooling in my mouth. "Stella had a restraining order against this guy? Did you find out why? Was he violent?"

Shaking her head, Nicki leaned in again. "My guy couldn't find out the reason, but he said whatever it was, it was probably nothing major since Stella dropped the whole thing a few months later."

My body reeled with unanswered questions. I wanted to shake Nicki and spill every detail out of her, but before I could bombard her, she tossed a navy blue backpack on the table and started cramming her things into it. As Nicki battled with her books, I reached into the large pocket on the front of my sweater and pulled out the only leverage I had.

"One last question," I said, flashing the pearl bracelet like it was a dirty little secret. "Ever see this before?"

Nicki's face scrunched up. "Ew. No." She frowned deeper.

"It's pearls," we both said in unison.

Rolling my eyes, I pushed away from the table and gave Nicki some space as she got ready to leave. The way she watched me gave me pause. If I didn't know any better, I'd have thought Nicki cared for my ghostly friend more than she wished to admit. I wondered how much of that was true for Stella as well. Relationships were intimidating, and it was looking like my very conceited familiar was no better than the rest of us.

For a very brief moment, I felt like I had won a small battle over Stella Rutherford. I may not have had the money or the closets full of the latest clothes, but my relationships, the few there were, were not based on falsities.

My phone vibrated in my hands as I left the restaurant, my body freezing when I saw the name on the Caller ID.

"Hi, Joe," I said as I picked up.

"Piper, glad I caught you," the vampire answered.

Scanning the parking lot, I caught sight of the same cab that drove me here parked in one of the spots and made a beeline for the car. "Is everything okay?" I asked.

"Definitely. Where are you?"

I looked back at the neon hot dog. "Coral Reef. I was right about to leave."

"Don't," Joe instructed. "I'll come pick you up."

Understanding and I were not friends. I looked at the short distance between myself and the cab and stopped walking. "It's okay. I can get a cab."

How did Joe even know I need a ride? I had no chance to dwell on it because he said, "You're not getting out of it this time, Piper Addison. I'm taking you on a proper date and I won't take no for an answer."

Then the man hung up.

I stood in the restaurant's parking lot with the phone pressed to my ear and a clouded look on my face. Joe was coming here to take me on a date. The same date we'd been trying to make for weeks. Then why wasn't I more excited?

Looking down at the patches of worn-out jeans on my leggings, I shook my head. Despite my eagerness to have dinner with the vampire, I could only think of one thing.

Stella Rutherford was never going to let me live this down.

CHAPTER 10

T his was not good. This was not good at all.

My fingernails dug half moons into the soft flesh of my palms as I walked across the lot with Joe beside me. The Cliffside Diner—the poshest place in Orchard Hollow—grew larger as we approached. I was suddenly all too aware of how underdressed I was. Walking next to me, Joe fit right in. Of course.

The evening was cool, as it often was at this time of year, but Joe seemed very comfortable in his button-up cardigan and jeans that did all the right things for his muscular thighs. I was so uncomfortable, I couldn't even drool over the vampire's lusciousness. What an epic waste of a great pair of pants.

Directly below us, the waves threw themselves into the cliffs and I peered out to the horizon line to see the sky change colors. Purples and reds and oranges painted the beach in beautiful shades as the sun set for the evening. Joe hurried as we neared the front doors. I stiffened.

"I don't think I'm dressed for this," I admitted, my cheeks burning with embarrassment.

At my words, Joe looked me up and down with a slight smirk tugging at his lips. "You look beautiful, as usual," he said. Then he removed his cardigan to reveal a raggedy T-shirt with his bookshop's logo on the front. "There, now we're both underdressed."

Chuckling, I waited until he opened the door for me to pass and ducked into the restaurant. Unlike the Coral Reef, Cliffside Diner was surprisingly quiet. The floor to ceiling windows to our left showcasing the town's most beautiful view of the sea weren't lined with patrons as they often were. I looked around, realizing quickly there was not one other person in the entire restaurant. It was only me and Joe. *Are they closed?* My head whipped back and forth in confusion. For as long as I lived here, I couldn't remember the diner ever closing. It was the spot to be; especially during the tourist season like the one we were currently in.

Joe stopped at the maître d' stand, looked at me and winked. "It's a surprise."

Before I could pummel the man with questions, a server in a stuffy-looking five-piece suit walked at a fast clip toward us. "Mr. Brooks! Welcome, welcome. We have a table ready for you, if you'll follow me."

The server spun on his heel and proceeded to speed walk toward the windows. I followed behind Joe at a brisk pace, my brow creasing.

"I know the owner," Joe said. "He owes me a favor. I figured what better way to use it than to treat you to a special night?"

If a human heart could physically tear out of someone's chest and slap them across the face, mine would have done it. I was still trying to wrap my head around the fact that Joe, who was fairly new in town, knew the owner of the diner, but that he thought it was worthwhile to waste a pretty special favor on me.

The server led us to a cozy table by the center window and my throat tightened as we approached. A lily-white tablecloth spread out over the table. Atop it, three candles of varying heights cast a serene glow over the otherwise dim restaurant interior. There was a bottle of very expensive Champagne chilling in an ice bucket beside the table and two plates were set opposite each other, waiting for the two of us. I blinked, pleasantly surprised. Joe thought of everything. The server said, "I'll be right back to take your order," as I squeezed into the chair Joe pulled out for me.

I looked at Joe over the glow of the candles. "This is amazing."

"It's nothing," he said, shaking his head.

"It's not nothing, Joe. It's the nicest thing anyone has ever done for me. Thank you."

The vampire grinned and lit up the room a million times more than the candles. "Travis was a client from back in the day," he explained. "I got him out of a sticky situation once that saved him a boatload of money. In case you're wondering what the favor was for."

"Good to know. For a second there, I thought you helped him bury a body."

Joe grinned teasingly. "I never said I didn't."

Taking out the napkin from my plate, I placed it on my lap and opened the menu. Everything in this place was so much more expensive than I could ever afford, and I got flashbacks to the last time I was here interrogating a possible murderer. My thoughts ran amuck, interrupted only by the sound of the Champagne bottle popping open. Joe poured out two glasses and waited for me to pick mine up. "I told Travis we might not order anything on the menu," he said. "His chef is more than happy to whip up a pizza if you'd prefer a less pretentious meal."

I thought back to the soggy pasta I never finished waiting for me at home. "Pizza sounds lovely, but I'd be happy with anything."

"Your happiness is my command, madam."

Feeling bolder, I took a sip of the Champagne and the bubbles fluttered in my stomach, making me giddier than a child on a hot summer day. When the server returned, Joe placed our order for the largest pizza the chef could create. As he handed off our menus, he quirked an eyebrow in my direction. I couldn't help but laugh again; the man had one heck of a fake appetite, which was great because I was starving. Vampires didn't need human food to survive, but they did pretend to have it to stay under the radar. That was one of the things the old stories actually got right. Not the burning in the sun part, though. That was all theatrics. Most of them also didn't go around draining humans of their blood and, like Joe, could survive of ethically sourced blood to stay alive. Of course there were still outliers. No one liked those monsters.

My stomach growled and I cringed.

The entire business with Nicki put me on edge and while I wasn't sure what the proper etiquette for a date was, I certainly couldn't wait to share everything I discovered about Stella's past life with Joe.

Though before I had the chance to speak, Joe spread his palms on the table and said, "I made more headway on the Sisters of the River."

My fingers tightened around the stem of the Champagne flute.

"What did you find out?" I asked, trying not to shatter the glass with my sudden Hulk strength. Joe shifted his weight in his seat, our feet touching under the table. My stomach jumped up into my throat. It wasn't the most romantic gesture, sure, but when you've been out of the dating circle as long as I have, a foot under a table was enough to get you going.

Downing the Champagne in my glass, I concentrated on calming down and gestured for Joe to continue.

"How much do you know about the coven your mother joined when she left here?" he asked.

Well, that'll do it. There was no space for romance where Sylvie Addison was concerned. I grimaced. "Nothing, really. Gran never told me much. I think she was trying to protect me," I answered. "All I know is that they practice dark magic and according to the letters I found in the attic, my mom knew them for a lot longer than Gran let on."

Across from me, Joe's Adam's apple bobbed up

and down, his eyes flaring. "Any chance the dark magic your grandmother told you about could be connected to the underworld? To Hades?"

The Champagne flute I held clinked against my plate, the sound echoing through the restaurant.

"I'm not sure," I replied. "If we're talking about dark magic, then the underworld is as dark as it gets. But why would my mom join a coven that worshipped such a demonic deity? It doesn't make sense."

"I thought so as well when I found out," Joe agreed.

My ears burnt. "How did you get this information? Sylvie didn't exactly leave a return address when she bounced."

"I paid a friend to track your mother's whereabouts."

The exclamation caught me off guard to the point that my teeth ground together. Joe paid someone to track my mom. That was extreme. More importantly, why didn't I think of it before? I felt instantly foolish, then tried to cram the thoughts down so I could keep my attention on my date and not on my own short-comings.

"Your mom is pretty good at staying off the radar, but my friend was able to find a connection between her and the Sisters of the River. At least up until the point they disappeared off the map."

My eyebrows arched so high they touched my hairline. "You can't seriously think that Sylvie is part of this mysterious coven. We don't even know if the Sisters of the River truly exist. They sound like a myth to me."

"Most things that ought to stay hidden tend to do so," Joe rebutted.

It was an excellent point. Paranormals have hidden in the shadows for centuries and the humans never caught on. What would make the Sisters of the River be any different? I mean, if we could convince the rest of the world that vampires and werewolves and warlocks and witches didn't exist, why not one measly little coven? My knees knocked together under the table. I guess that could explain why Mom never came home. You couldn't make a coven vanish from existence if you're sending postcards to your family.

A large, steaming tray of pizza appeared at our table and the smell of warm cheese pierced my nostrils. I sighed blissfully, wiping the drool that was likely forming on the edges of my mouth. Joe thanked the server, asking him to deliver a second bottle of Champagne, even though we were making slow headway through the one we had, then cut us a few slices each. I reached for the hot sauce bottle at the same time as him. As our fingers grazed, both of us jerked our hands away. I giggled, going for the bottle again before Joe had a chance to snatch it out of my reach. Date or not, no one was standing between me and my hot sauce.

Patting the back of the bottle, I started to squeeze some onto my pizza when the thing exploded in my hand. Hot sauce attacked me from every angle. A burning sensation started in my right eye and I pressed my palm to it, rubbing the pain away. *You have got to be kidding me! Did I just hot sauce myself on a date with Joe?* My clumsiness had no limits. I wanted to play the whole thing off, but the pain was getting worse. If I didn't wash the stupid thing out, I might lose an eye.

"Are you all right?"

"Eye. Burning. Hot," I mumbled like an imbecile.

Hand digging into my purse, I scrambled around the bottom, feeling triumphant when my fingers closed around the eye drops I kept there. I brought the dropper to my eye, eager to get this nightmare over with. If my vision returned, I could turn this date around.

"You should hold off on the drops," Joe cautioned.

It was too late; I already had half the bottle dripping into my burning eyeball. That was a terrible, terrible mistake. The combination of eye drops and hot sauce was something they should warn you about in health class. The pain intensified to a point I thought I might scream. My entire body was now feeling like it was on fire. I couldn't see at all and fumbled with my hands, the eye drop bottle falling to the floor. As I reached for it, my head collided with something hard.

"Ow!" Joe yelped. *Great. Now I'm taking him down with me.* Joe pushed a glass of water my way. "Here, have some water."

Foolishly, I tried to brush him off because the last thing I needed was more water. As I did so, my palm slapped his hand and water spilled everywhere. Now I was on fire and soaking wet. A truly wonderful combination.

While I battled the personal hell I was in, the server manifested out of thin air beside us. "Is everything all right here?"

"Yes!" I yelled at the same time as Joe said, "No. Can you bring us a wet napkin, please?"

I leaned back in my chair, wishing I was better at magic so I could spell myself invisible. When the server returned, I pressed the wet napkin against my eye, battling the urge to rub it.

"Hold it there and keep blinking. It'll pass," Joe said.

"Are you sure?" I asked, panting. "And also, how do you know what to do in this very specific situation?"

Joe smiled, or at least I thought he did, because my

vision was still spotty. "You're not the only one here who's had that experience."

Our solidarity in this disgusting affair did not make me feel any better, yet Joe was correct. While it felt like forever and a day, it took only a few more moments for the pain in my eye to subside and my sight to return. I lowered the napkin into my lap, soaking my leggings. "Tell me the truth," I said. "Do I look like a proper leper?"

"As I told you earlier, you look beautiful, as usual."

Stifling the embarrassment I felt earlier, I grinned from ear to ear. "Careful, Mr. Brooks," I teased. "If you keep up the flatteries, I might think you're sweet on me."

"Challenge accepted," Joe joked. "Now how about we forget about the hot sauce, and secret covens, and you can tell me more about your life growing up here? I'd love to know what crazy adventures you got up to in this town."

We spent the rest of the evening talking about joyful, happy things. I told Joe about my childhood and Gran. He spoke of his life in the city. How he became a lawyer. When he decided he needed a simpler life, and moved here. We talked for hours until the sun set over the water and the sea turned into a dark, deep void beyond the windows.

When we finished the last drop of the second

Champagne bottle, Joe left the server a hefty tip and we made our way back to his car. The door of the restaurant closed behind us as I walked toward the vehicle. Suddenly, I felt a tug on my wrist pulling me back. I turned to see Joe holding my hand, his eyes twinkling in the low light of the moon. He leaned in closer. And closer. And closer. My eyes darted around the lot to make sure we were alone and weren't about to get bombarded by my familiar again. When I saw the coast was clear, I leaned in too. Our lips collided. Joe tasted like peppermint, and my legs buckled under my weight. Joe wrapped a strong arm around my waist and pulled me into him until there was no space between us. The kiss was the best kiss of my life. If not for Joe pulling away with a boyish grin on his face, I'd have stayed there with him forever.

"I had a great time tonight," he whispered against my brow.

I bit the inside of my cheek. "Me too."

"Let's do this again," Joe added, "and soon."

"How does tomorrow morning sound to you?"

Pulling away from me, Joe tightened his lips and cocked his head to the side. "What are you up to now, Piper Addison?"

"I may or may not have done some digging online for Stella's ex-fiancé while waiting for you to pick me up tonight." I tucked a loose strand of hair behind my ear.

"And?"

"And he works as a security guard in a small casino in the city," I said. "Want to come with me to check him out?"

This was the moment Joe would normally tell me to drop it and to play it safe. Except this time, he didn't. Instead, the vampire shook his head and pulled me in closer, his breath hot on my head. "Not exactly the date I had in mind, but sure."

It was my turn to pull away. "Really?"

"Yep," Joe said. "I think we both know you're going with or without me, at least this way I get to keep you company for the drive over. I'll pick you up first thing in the morning."

My arm looped around his and as we made our way to the car, I tried not to pass out from excitement. *Keep breathing. Keep breathing. Keep breathing.* We were almost at the doors when the hairs on the back of my neck stood straight. I turned, looking over my shoulder. The parking lot was empty except for one car that likely belonged to our server, yet I had the distinct feeling that we were being watched. My body bristled and my heart rate sped up as I clung tighter to Joe. Out of the corner of my eye, I thought I saw a flash of movement, but when I double checked, there was no one there. Only me and Joe.

On the ride home I tried not to think about the strange, ominous feeling I had in the lot, choosing instead to concentrate on the perfect date I had with one sexy vampire and how I couldn't wait to rub Stella's nose in it.

CHAPTER 11

Stella Rutherford

P iper and the bloodsucker sat in the center window of the Cliffside Diner, their faces lit up by the candles between them. In all honesty, it appeared to be a fabulous date. The bloodsucker put on the good show. Who would have thought?

I floated beyond the windows, biding my time in the shadows and watching Piper on the date. She seemed to be having a great time aside from that wretched hot sauce incident, which came as no surprise to me. Our girl was as accident prone as they came. In fact, I was pleasantly surprised she hadn't yet burned the place down with those candles. The little witch was coming around; maybe she'd learned a thing or two from me.

My long ponytail wavered in the wind and I glanced down at the sea beneath me. *The one good thing about being dead,* I thought, looking around. *The views are unbeatable.*

Behind the thick glass, the vampire said something and Piper burst into laughter, her body shaking like that of a deranged goose. *Heavens, no. Control yourself.* I knew the vamp had a crush on her, but she could at least keep some mystery. I frowned, taking in her choice of outfit. It was most definitely not Stella-approved.

Rubbing the bridge of my nose, I flattened out my brow before it creased. No one liked a wrinkly ghost and heaven knows I didn't spend all that money when I was alive, only to get wrinkles in my afterlife. My body felt heavy. I looked down at my arm, seeing right through it all the way to the water below. Every time I received bad news, my "body" did this. It was frustrating how often it failed me and I could do nothing to change it. Trapped in the incessant shell for all of eternity. With hair that hasn't been washed in two days and this awful tennis attire. I didn't even enjoy tennis that much; I only went for the martinis and the gossip. Arthur constantly asked me to quit, but I would hear nothing of it.

"A Rutherford does not quit, dear," I would tell him.

He'd laugh and give me a peck on the forehead before rushing off to work. For someone his age, the man was a workhorse. It was one of the things I loved most about him: his work ethic was close to that of my own.

Not that I had to work once we got together.

Arthur changed my life, and I would never find a way to repay him. Especially not now that I was dead.

The frown lines returned when I remembered the hole I was in before becoming a Rutherford.

It was strange. I hadn't thought of Sam once in the time I'd been dead, not until Nicki mentioned him. *Hiring a private investigator to split up her father and me... That awful, ungrateful girl!* And to think I actually considered her family. Goes to show you can never trust anyone.

I glanced through the window of the restaurant again and watched as Joe pulled Piper's chair out, the date seemingly coming to an end.

I supposed I could trust the witch; she proved herself to be loyal and a true friend to me time and time again. Which was exactly why she could never know the truth.

Piper was getting too close.

I knew her by now and she would dig and dig and dig until she found out everything. And then what would happen? Piper would never speak to me again if she knew what happened with Sam.

Even the thought of him made my skin break out in a cold sweat. Arthur didn't just change my life, he saved me. Saved me from the path I was on, saved me from myself.

I needed to think of a plan, and fast. What else could Piper uncover next? I couldn't risk her knowing anything.

Could she leave me? I wondered. How did the familiar bond work for witches when they no longer wanted you around? *No matter.*

I bristled, rolling my shoulders to stand up straighter or float straighter in my case. Our bond could not break, *would* not break. I wouldn't allow for it.

Eyes narrowed, I watched Piper and the vampire exit the restaurant, cramming my nearly invisible body into the darkest corners of the parking lot. My eyes slipped away when the vamp finally made his move and gave Piper a kiss I knew I would hear a lot about later. I was happy for her and a part of me was even pleased that she wanted so badly to help me. But another part, a darker part had to steer her away.

My gaze followed the car as it pulled out of the lot, heart sinking. To protect Piper, I had to do the one thing I never wanted to do.

I had to lie to my best friend.

CHAPTER 12

I t was dark out when Joe picked me up in the morning; the encroaching winter swallowing the town in gloom one day at a time. I snuck out of the house, careful not to disturb Harry in whatever hole he was hiding in. The last thing I wanted was to wrestle snacks out of the furry thief's hands and make Joe wait for me. Especially considering he was nice enough to entertain my theatrics and drive all the way out to the city.

I glanced around the quiet farmhouse. No sign of Stella. The ghost hadn't popped in last night, nor was she anywhere to be found this morning. Unusual behavior for her. I would have thought she'd be all over me for details on yesterday's date. And if I were being honest, I was a tad disappointed I didn't get to see her before leaving.

The date with Joe was the only action I'd gotten in years and I wanted someone to share in the excitement with.

Checking one last time for Stella, I locked up and skipped down the porch steps toward Joe's car. My belly fluttered when I spotted him leaning against the hood, his corduroy jacket unzipped. I pulled on my handmade scarf, tightening it around my neck to keep the frigid air from freezing me solid. Not all of us were of the vampire variety and, unlike Joe, I was an icicle by the time I reached the end of the driveway.

Joe flashed me a row of pearly whites. "Good morning. Have a good sleep?"

"I sure did," I said, ignoring his wiggling eyebrows.

Joe leaned in for a kiss at the same time as I turned to fix my dumb scarf again and his lips grazed my ear. I jerked my head around, our noses crashing together. Eye splitting pain shot up my face and I yelped, horror crawling its way up my body. Was my entire relationship with Joe going to be one accident away from broken bones?

Were we even in a relationship?

Joe chuckled, rubbing the tip of his reddened nose. He reached behind him and produced an extra-large coffee cup, then handed it to me. "We'll try that again after you've had this."

Cradling the drink to my chest, I sheepishly made my way around the car and poured myself into the passenger seat. My ears flushed and the pain behind my eyes from our collision made me see double. Though that could have been my soul rejecting my clumsy body as a host.

While Joe settled in for the long drive, I checked the mirror to make sure I didn't break anything, relieved to discover not a single bruise. I took a long sip, warmth creeping to my face. "Apple spiced latte?" I arched an eyebrow at Joe. "Did you stop by Bean Me Up?"

"I may have," he answered, backing out of the driveway. "Rory says to tell you she's got everything under control."

My fingers curled around the door handle. "Oh, no. How much of a disaster was it?"

"The place was actually in good shape. And she got through the morning rush without spilling anything." Joe's hands hiked up briefly to give me a thumbs up. "It's good of you to give her more responsibility. Rory's a good kid."

My tense back relaxed, and I melted into the heated seats of Joe's car. As excited as I was to take this day trip, I was a nervous wreck over leaving Rory at the cafe on her own. Cilia, her aunt, promised to check in on the hot mess express that was my employee, but it did little to calm me down. There was a lot of damage the young witch could do in one day, and I worried I might return to a massive disaster later. Hearing Joe describe the cafe as being in good hands helped erase some of those doubts. And it was true, Rory could use the alone hours running the place. The kid had to learn to take control one way or another.

"Did you go to Bean Me Up to check up on her?" I asked Joe.

He chuckled sneakily. "It's possible," he answered. "I figured you would be crawling out of your skin. The latte was a good bonus, though. On the house, apparently."

"Oh, geez. I wonder how many on the house drinks Rory is giving out today."

Joe's laughter was contagious and soon I joined him, our giggles filling the car. We zoomed down the empty, wide road between the mountains that took us away from Orchard Hollow and into the world beyond. My eyes narrowed on the sign letting us know we were leaving town and to come again soon. I couldn't remember the last time I'd visited the city. Actually, come to think of it, I couldn't recall when I last left Orchard Hollow at all.

I was pretty sure I hadn't locked eyes on that sign for years, definitely not since Gran passed away.

"Did you get anything out of Stella about this Sam character?"

My jumbled thoughts scrambled to make sense in my head as I stared out the window. "You know, I couldn't find her anywhere," I admitted. "She wasn't around last night or this morning. It's odd."

"Harry Houdini still there?" Joe asked.

I nodded.

"She's probably avoiding him. You said she's been nagging you to get rid of the raccoon, right?"

Another nod and I was back to staring out the window as the scenery changed. The mountains dispersed, taking us farther and farther away from home. Soon, even the clusters of trees would thin out as we'd near the city.

My forehead rested on the glass as Joe maneuvered the winding road, eyes suddenly heavy with sleep. We jerked to a stop and the loud honk of a horn stunned me awake. My eyes flew open, two red lights staring me straight in the face.

"Welcome to King City," Joe said.

I rubbed the sleep from my eyes. "Sorry, I dozed off. I'm the worst road-trip partner ever."

"Don't think anything of it. Glad you got some sleep," Joe said warmly. "So, where to?"

Bending over, I dug into the purse at my feet and reached for my phone. While getting ready, I pulled up the address for the casino I tracked Sam to online. "The Lucky Stars Casino on Richmond Street," I told Joe. "You know it?"

"Sure do. It's not the best neighborhood, so let's keep this short."

Agreeing, I watched the city unfold in the front window as Joe turned right and left, expertly zooming down the narrow streets. The casino must have been located on one of the busier intersections; there were so many people on the street I had trouble making out their faces. I knew Joe said the neighborhood was off, but it didn't look any different from all the other streets we drove by. A fight broke out between two rough-looking men while we waited at a red light.

Right. Make it fast. Got it.

A few more blocks and Joe parallel parked behind a beat-up convertible that's seen better days, and walked out, opening the door for me to climb out. As he sped away, I hauled myself after him, eyes darting up and down the street. Suddenly, Joe made a sharp right turn into an alley.

I slowed my step. "Are you sure you know where you're going?"

"Unfortunately, yes," Joe replied. "I had a few clients I had to meet at this place."

Joe's legal career was starting to look a lot less glamorous than it did before. The deeper we walked into the alley, the happier I became I didn't make the trip alone. Bringing a vampire as my backup may have been one of the smarter things I did this year.

Joe came to an abrupt stop, and I bumped into his wide back with an oomph. Slowly, I peered out from behind him, spotting a shifty door in the midst of a wall of brick. Above it, the name Lucky Stars flickered in neon blue with an obnoxious arrow pointing down. There was a man leaning against the door. Both he and the wood appeared to have the same amount of decomposition.

Scowling, Joe tapped the man on the shoulder. When he looked up, his eyes barely focused as he grunted under his breath before walking the opposite of a straight line down the alley.

Drunk before noon. Lovely.

I considered telling Joe that I changed my mind and we should return home, but he had the door open before I had the chance. My curiosity got the better of me, and I followed him down the dingy stairs into the deep recesses of my own personal hell.

The Lucky Stars Casino was more dive bar than gambling nook. To our right, a bronze-cast bar ran the length of the wall. Shelves on the exposed brick displayed bottles of liquor and dusty glassware. The bar top looked like it hadn't been wiped since before the Revolution and there were already piles of dirty glasses waiting to be picked up even though it was still technically the morning.

Beyond the bar and tighter to the left were the slot machines, and next to those, several poker tables. The casino, a loose word to be used for this place, housed a stage at the rear upon which the saddest set of drums, an amp, and a mic stand collected more dust than the bar top. An older gentleman with long, oily hair and a blue bandana sang a rough tune I didn't recognize. Singing was also a loose word for what was happening on stage.

Despite it being very early, there were already several people slumped over the tables and in the slot machine chairs.

I looked at Joe and he raised a brow, taking a step closer toward me. "I told you," he said. "It's a rough place."

We huddled together as we made our way past the main area of the casino and toward the back rooms. Joe mentioned the last time he was here and dealing with the manager, he saw a security office, which he bet Sam would be in if he was on shift. I kept a careful watch on the staggering drunks as we walked, thinking security was definitely required here. Though everyone seemed to be too incapacitated to get rowdy.

Actually, a couple of the fine patrons of the casino seemed like they had been here since the night before.

I dodged a man's drink as it wobbled off the table and fell to the floor, the glass rolling and splashing the smelly concoction that filled it all over the place. If Sam wasn't on shift, I'd feel absolutely awful for dragging Joe to this place.

We reached the door to the right of the stage and Joe gave it a hard knock, his arms crossed as he peered into the frosted glass panel in the center. A shadow zoomed behind the glass and as it crept closer, the shape of a man began to take form. Soon, the sound of locks unlocking filled my ears, and the door handles twisted back and forth. After a few more attempts, the door swung open, revealing a tall, muscular man in a tan security uniform. The man had finger-brushed black hair streaked with gray and a thick, well-trimmed beard in similar shades. His brown eyes narrowed, crinkling in the corners, as he took us in. My own eyes flicked to the name badge on his left pocket. Bingo!

"Oh, no," Sam said with a huff. "You here to file a complaint? Manager's not in until noon."

Joe shook his head. "Not at all."

"We're here to talk to you, actually," I added.

Confusion laced Sam's features as he rolled his eyes over Joe and me slowly. His hand came up to rest on the holster at his hip, which I assumed did not hold a bag of Skittles. I swallowed hard, pressing into Joe's side.

"Not here to cause any trouble," Joe said. "Piper was a friend of someone you knew. We promise we won't keep you long."

"Stella Rutherford," I said quickly. "I believe you two were quite close."

Sam's hand drifted off the holster, fingers relaxing at his side. "You don't say," he muttered. "I haven't talked to Stella in ages. But I knew her as Stella McGuire. How's she doing, anyway?"

"Not great." I coughed lightly. "She died."

The man's face changed instantly. The worry lines on his brow deepened into thick wrinkles and his mouth down turned, making him appear like a sad puppy dog. He closed a palm over his lips, rubbing at his beard until the skin under the stubble turned red.

"Stella's dead?" he asked, his voice cracking.

I tucked in my chin and said, "Yes. Sorry to be the one to bring the bad news. Do you think we can talk somewhere in private real quick?"

"Of course," Sam answered. He stepped aside, and I followed Joe through the doorway. "We can talk in my office."

As we walked down the narrow hallway leading to Sam's office, I was pleasantly surprised that the rear of the establishment was a direct opposite to the main area. No drunks littered the corridor, it was quiet enough I could hear myself think, and it even smelled better back here—like lilacs and brown sugar.

Sam stopped in front of a steel door and reached into his back pocket to pull out a set of keys. He fumbled with the lock a few times before it finally gave and the door opened. The room behind it was a plain gray cube with one desk, three chairs, and a dusty old computer. Sam skirted around the desk, sucking in to squeeze between it and the wall, then motioned toward the other two chairs.

"So, you were Stella's friend," he muttered. "In Orchard Hollow, I take it?"

"Uh-huh. She mentioned you two were engaged for a bit," I said.

Beside me, Joe bristled and Sam mirrored his motions.

"Hmm," the guard mused, rubbing his chin again. His lips parted, and I noticed an empty space where one of his front teeth should be. When he caught me staring, he said, "Job can get tough. And yeah, Stella and I wanted to tie the knot, but it never happened."

"Because she met Arthur."

Sam's toothy grin vanished. "Yep. Some old dude in a small town, who'd have thought?"

I tucked my hands under my thighs and

exchanged a quick glance with Joe. Turning my attention back to Sam, I said, "Must have gutted you that Stella left you for him."

"You have no idea," Sam answered. "I thought we had something good, that we were solid, you know? But she kicked me to the curb without a second thought. That was Stella for you."

He wasn't all wrong. When I first met Stella, she wasn't exactly nice and cuddly. Come to think of it, she was a block of ice at times. But she was my block, and I loved her for it.

"What do you mean by that?" Joe asked.

"Oh, just that she was always working an angle," Sam replied. "Did you know I followed her to Orchard Hollow? When I first found out she ditched me for the Crypt Keeper."

My lips tightened. I did not know that at all, and Stella hadn't mentioned it. I wondered if she remembered this part of her past or if it was gone into the void of lost memories like the rest of her life.

"She never said anything to me," I admitted.

Sam opened and closed a drawer under the desk, his weight shifting in the creaking office chair. "I don't know what I was thinking. Any other guy would have cursed her name and moved on," he explained. "But I loved the stubborn woman, and I was intent on winning her back."

"Did you?"

"Hell no," he said. The disappointment on his face deepened, and he sighed, his eyes downcast. "Stella wanted nothing to do with me. At first, I thought she was after the guy's money, you know Stella, but I was wrong. She really loved the old fart."

"Why were you so convinced she was after his money?" I asked.

"Stella liked to scheme," he said. "Not sure if she told you how we met, but I brought her in at one of my old gigs."

My jaw unhinged. "Are you saying you arrested Stella at a casino?"

Sam chuckled and motioned over his uniform. "I'm not a cop," he said. "I can't arrest people."

"What then?"

"Stella was trying to get one over at a casino I worked in. Her and her friend Valerie had been plotting it for months. Little did they know, I was on to them from the start. Stella was hard to miss in a crowd, if you catch my drift."

That I did.

Pressing my back into the chair, I asked, "Do you know if this was the first time the two of them attempted to trick a casino?"

"I think so," Sam answered right as the phone on the desk rang. He picked it up, mumbling, "Be right there" before turning back to me. "Listen, sorry to rush you out, but I need to handle a situation out front."

"No problem," I said. "Thank you for talking to us. If you hear from Valerie, let me know. I'd love to ask her some questions too."

He reached into his desk drawer and pulled out a business card, sliding it across the table toward me. "Feel free to call me if you have any more questions. I'll see what I can find out for you on my end. I haven't heard from Valerie in some time and I doubt she'd do anything to hurt Stella."

I blanched. "Oh, I ain't implying that."

"No need to beat around the bush," Sam said. "I'm good at reading people. Also part of the job. I can tell you're trying to find out what happened to your friend and I'm happy to help in any way I can. Stella was important to me, I want to do right by her."

With that, he stood and walked to the door, waiting for us to follow. We started for the front, but Sam stopped us. "Take the back exit," he instructed. "It could get ugly out there."

I tried not to think about what that could mean as Sam stalked away from us toward the main casino. A few moments later, Joe was ushering me out the back door into yet another alley. Soon, we were in the car and on our way out of the city, leaving the casino in the dust. My mind reeled as we wove through the streets, recounting the conversation with Sam. There was so much I didn't know about Stella's past; so many unanswered questions.

Her amnesia didn't help piece the puzzle together.

Geez, Stella. How am I supposed to help you when there are gaping holes in the story?

I wanted to close my eyes and push the thoughts away, but a blue glow outside caught my attention. Blood pumped in my veins and my legs tensed as I saw the rip in the air approach the car at an escalating speed. We were driving right into it!

"Joe! Watch out!" I yelled to get his attention.

It was probably not the best idea to yell at someone behind the wheel. Joe's body jerked, and the wheel spun to the right, taking the car and us with it. His eyes focused on the rip, mouth gaping. In less than a second, Joe's vampire abilities kicked into gear, and he moved at lightning speed to recover the car's trajectory. The tires squealed as we swerved, barely avoiding a head on collision with a parked truck.

My lungs burned, and I sucked in a massive gulp of air when Joe got us back on the road. Swiveling in the seat, I turned to look out the back window, the rip nowhere in sight.

"What was that?" Joe asked.

My gaze flicked to the rearview mirror, the truck we nearly hit getting smaller as we drove away. That was a close call. We were almost involved in a serious car accident. What if that was a person walking and not a truck? My heart stopped.

I rubbed my eyes with the rear of my palms. "I'll tell you in a second. I need to make a phone call."

"To whom?"

Holding up a finger, I pulled out my phone, collected myself, and dialed a familiar number. "I might have a theory about Stella's cause of death."

CHAPTER 13

"**W**hy do you think that?" Romero asked, the aggravation evident in his gruff voice. "Coroner confirmed Mrs. Rutherford died from head trauma caused by a fall."

Biting my bottom lip, I tried to think of a way to explain to the sheriff what gave me the idea without sounding absolutely unhinged. I couldn't mention the accident we nearly got into that sparked the thought and I most definitely did not wish to tell Romero anything about the rips in the air or my increasingly unstable magic. He'd never trust me again, and I might need him for help with Stella's case. Not that he'd been particularly useful thus far.

"Call it a hunch," I said, settling on a semi-truth.

The sheriff sighed audibly, and I cringed. *Here we go.* "It isn't that your hunches have not been useful," he said. I could hear his teeth grinding on the line like he was standing right next to me. "But this time, I'm afraid you're wrong. Your friend's death, from all appearances, was an accident. Besides, there are no roads anywhere near that site."

"Is it possible she got hit, then stumbled away and fell?" I guessed. Why was I stuck on a hit and run so badly? I had no clue. There was a good chance I was projecting from my own near death experience, but I couldn't let it go. "I was there recently and the closest entrance to that part of the trails was near a very winding road. Hard to see a car coming from around the turn."

In the driver's seat, Joe tapped a finger on the wheel and waited patiently for me to finish. He parked in an abandoned lot near one of the bridges so I could make the call without the sound of rushing traffic in the background. Now, the surrounding silence was starting to get on my nerves.

"I'm going to regret asking this, Miss Addison, but did you see anything on those trails other than a supposedly deadly road?"

My lips twitched, the corners perking up. "Did I use my special skills, you mean?"

Next to me, Joe barked out a laugh, and I slapped his shoulder.

"Yes, that is what I mean," the sheriff huffed out. "I'm at the station, so let's keep the details to a minimum."

Continuing to grin, I said, "No problem. And you should know, no way magic was used to kill Stella. The area is infested with Belladonna; it's basically magical Kryptonite."

"An accident, Miss Addison."

Goosebumps crawled up my arms as I realized I was keeping a very big piece of evidence from the sheriff, one that might change his mind about the case. While I had my reservations when it came to working with the police, Romero was a good guy and I knew he'd do the right thing here. I fidgeted in the seat, stalling. "I did find something you might want to see," I finally said. "A bracelet buried in the woods nor far from the cliff. I'll bring it by when I'm back in town."

"A bracelet?" Romero asked, then quickly added, "Where are you, exactly?"

Darting my eyes like a toddler caught drawing on a wall, I glanced at Joe briefly before saying, "Sorry, gotta go! I'll try to swing by tonight or tomorrow morning at the latest."

Then I hung up.

Heat flashed over my neck and cheeks and I swallowed a large lump as I pocketed my cell phone.

"Did you hang up on the sheriff?" Joe asked.

I winced. "It's possible. Pretend that never happened." Head rolling back, I looked through the open window, the autumn air whipping at my face. From here, King City wasn't quite as intimidating. The bridge leading out of the city stretched over the sea, beckoning me to return home. And yet I couldn't. Not yet, anyway.

Turning to Joe, I asked, "Any chance I can interest you in staying for another couple of hours?"

"Are you thinking of lunch?"

"She's thinking she wants to stalk one of my oldest friends."

I screamed. Stella's voice from the backseat had my heartbeat shooting from zero to holy-crap-I'm-going-to-die in under sixty seconds. Neck almost breaking from turning around, I deadpanned at my familiar. "Stella! I told you to stop sneaking up on me. What are you doing here?"

"Darling, please, did you truly think you could harass my ex-fiancé and I wouldn't want to hear about it?" she asked. "Tell me what that sexy son of a biscuit had to say about me? Did he break down when you told him I'm dead? Did he cry?" She wiggled her shoulders to an invisible happy tune. "Please tell me he cried."

"Um, well..." I looked at Joe. "Stella's here. And no, Sam didn't cry. He was upset, understandably, but no waterworks. Did you expect him to?"

The ghost shrugged. "It would have been nice to know I was dearly missed."

"You are dearly missed, weirdo," I told her. "Anyway, since you're here and obviously reading my mind, think you can help us find your friend, Valerie? I figure since we're already in the city, we might as well scope her out."

My lips zipped shut before I mentioned what Sam told me about Stella's less than law-abiding past. I knew I had to ask her about it, but I didn't want to do it with Joe around. I had a hunch that was a conversation better had behind closed doors where I could contain Stella's over the top reaction should she have one. One thing I knew about my familiar was she did not appreciate being called out and putting her on the spot about her casino schemes would do exactly that.

That didn't mean I wasn't going to grill the truth out of her as soon as we got home.

"If you want any chance of finding Valerie," Stella said, "you'll need to find Chris."

I leaned over the front seat. "Who's Chris?"

"Valerie's boyfriend. At least he was ten years ago

when we were on speaking terms." Stella held up a gray finger. "Don't ask me what happened, I don't know even know myself. We lost touch, I suppose. Anyhow, she was in love with that sad excuse for a man. I wouldn't put it past her to have married the loser."

Nodding, I turned around toward Joe. "Can you look up a Chris...what's his last name?"

"Meadow. Christopher Meadow."

"Meadow," I told Joe. "Is there an address listed somewhere?"

Pulling out his phone, Joe typed while I kept my attention on Stella. She was trying very hard to look unbothered, but I knew her by now. Something was eating away at the ghost and I intended to find out what it was. I hadn't seen Stella this unnerved since the time Harry jumped through her. Speaking of...

"Is Harry okay at home?" I asked.

Stella rolled her eyes aggressively. "He dug up the garden and left muddy prints all over your couch," she answered. "So, yes. He's his usual self."

My mouth gaped, and I was about to tell the ghost off for not leading with that priceless bit of information when Joe said, "Got it."

Starting the car, he backed us out onto the main road and sped away. The wind whipped my hair over my face, the streets blurring in my periphery. Soon, the skyscrapers dispersed, and we found ourselves surrounded by two-story buildings. Storefronts, most of which were boarded up, lined the street we drove on. Above them, decrepit windows and peeling paint outlined apartments that were as livable as a sewer. I couldn't picture anyone calling one of those units their home.

"Are you sure this is the right area?" I asked.

"Positive," Joe answered.

Behind us, Stella scoffed. "Leave it to Chris to live in this fresh hell. Man could never get a grasp on a savings account."

Maneuvering around a garbage pile, Joe pulled up to the curb to park. I ducked my head to glance outside and tried to gauge which one of the hovels upstairs belonged to Valerie's boyfriend. It didn't matter. They all looked equally unappealing.

We climbed out and Joe led the way to a metal door next to a closed convenience store. He straightened his collar, reading out the names on the buzzer. "There he is," Joe said, tapping the buzzer for number five.

Joe must have pressed the dumb thing twenty times before someone answered.

"Hello?" a rough voice sounded on the intercom. "Who's there?"

I stiffened. "Oh, hi, hello there. Are you Mr. Meadow?"

"Is this a joke?"

Raising one eyebrow at Joe, I mouthed, "What?" He responded with a shrug. "No joke, sir," I told the voice. "We're trying to track down someone he knows, Valerie Thomas. She was a friend of a friend."

"You're not debt collectors, are you?"

Again, what?

"Not at all," I answered. My eyes jumped to Stella, but she remained by Joe's car and didn't seem to care about the bizarre conversation. "Do you know if Christopher is home?"

The intercom went silent. I was certain we lost the guy, whoever he was. A few seconds later, there was a beep, and the voice said, "Look, I'll tell you the same thing I told the last people who came by. I haven't seen that piece of work in almost a decade. The guy skipped out on his rent and vanished into thin air, him and his girl. Bunch of no good tenants." He coughed and spit on the line. Chills crept up my body. "I don't know what your business is with him or the girlfriend, and I don't care. You won't find him here."

Taken aback by his hostility, I teetered backward, stopping only when Joe's hand pressed to my lower back. "Okay. Well, thank you, anyway," I said, even though I wasn't sure what I was thanking him for.

"If you find Chris, tell him I want my money," the voice said and hung up.

The intercom beeped a few times, then the line went dead, leaving Joe and me standing on the street in silence. I looked around, the eeriness of the empty street making me want to run away. The place was a ghost town. Somehow, I doubted the rude man on the phone—the building's owner, I assumed—had very many people interested in renting the place. No wonder he was upset.

Deflated, I spun on my heel and stalked toward the car and Stella. The ghost looked completely out of it and I wondered why she was acting this way, considering it was her death I was investigating. At this point, I didn't know who was more rude, my familiar or the absolute nightmare on the intercom.

"He's not here," I told her. "The owner hadn't seen him in years."

Stella blew out a short breath. "That tracks quite well for Chris," she told me. "Valerie talked about moving south. Perhaps they finally got around to it."

Conveniently enough when we were looking for them? I didn't buy it. Why would Stella's friend disappear ten years ago, right around the time Stella died? If that was a coincidence, I was a skilled witch. I laughed to myself. I had more of a chance of becoming an Olympic skater than getting the handle on my magic.

I was still giggling when Stella said, "Forget Chris. I know who you should talk to next."

Nodding at Joe to let him know I'll fill him in later, I asked Stella, "Who?"

"You need to get back to Orchard Hollow immediately," she instructed. "Find Fouster, Arthur's business partner."

Head spinning, I attempted to make sense of what Stella said. Since when did Arthur have a business partner? And why didn't she mention him before? I had no time to ask because Stella said, "I remembered another detail while you were chatting. I remember arguing with Fouster. It felt heated."

"Do you remember what it was about?"

She shook her head. "No," Stella replied. "But I do remember his angry face right before he pushed me. You need to talk to him, Piper. There's a chance I've recalled the exact moment I died."

Bile rolled up my throat. *Well, crap.*

CHAPTER 14

Gravel crunched under the wheels as Joe turned into my driveway. Behind us, the reddened sky reflected in the rearview mirror. I sighed as the farmhouse appeared ahead, ready to call it a night.

Somewhere between King City and home, Stella vanished, so it was only Joe and me in the car now. He parked and left the engine running while I zipped up my jacket. The walk from the car to the front door was short, but I could already feel the crisp air of the late afternoon seep into my bones.

"You're probably sick of me by now, but how about dinner later?" Joe asked.

His arm draped over the passenger side seat and as

I brushed up against it, the smell of his cologne drew me closer. My muscles tensed, anticipation thrumming through me. "I'm not at all sick of you," I answered. "Dinner sounds great. I'm going to pop into Bean Me Up to check on Rory and help her close up. How does eight sound?"

"Sounds perfect," Joe said. He leaned in, placing the softest of kisses on my lips, then pulled away. I tried not to scowl when the space between us expanded. "I'll bring takeout."

Taking my sweet time, I thanked him for accompanying me today and climbed out of the car, waving goodbye as Joe peeled out of the driveway. When he was out of sight, I skirted around the farmhouse to check on the mess in the garden Stella mentioned earlier. When I reached the cobblestone path leading from the rear of the house to the greenhouse, my jaw slacked. Gran's garden was in shambles. Every flower had been dug up and ripped to shreds and the few pots that survived lay on their side, abandoned mid-attack. The clicking of nails on wood sounded around the side of the greenhouse as I set off down the path.

"Harry Houdini!" I yelled, fist in the air.

My feet pummeled the stones, and I bolted for the raccoon, who hung off an open greenhouse window. His chubby behind swayed like a pendulum while the troublemaker attempted to scramble through the window to get inside.

"Don't you even think about it!" I screeched, sliding in beside him.

Having no time to make a rational decision, I grabbed Harry's furry body and pulled. The raccoon hissed and kicked out his hind legs, one of his paws slapping me on the cheek.

"Ouch!" I yelled. The little monster was in a serious need of a pedicure. "Get your sorry self out of there this instant!"

I pulled again, avoiding his razor-sharp nails and making a mental note to get checked for rabies later. Finally, I managed to get Harry off the window. He dropped to the ground, hissing as he wobbled away from me and toward the house. The back door creaked and slammed shut, Harry disappearing from view.

Freaking magician.

Shaking my head in aggravation, I walked to the front, hoping I wouldn't regret leaving Harry alone in the house later. A yawn escaped me as I backed the Beetle out of the driveway and headed for Cliff Row. I couldn't wait to have another coffee. Fingers crossed, the cafe was still standing by the time I got there because I didn't have it in me to deal with any of Rory's possible disasters.

The sea was angry today, the waves crashing into

the rocks as I drove the mountain road into town. I glanced out of the side window at the whitecaps in the distance. *Looks like another storm is coming.* When I brought my eyes back to the road, a sense of dread filled me. My eyes flicked to the rearview mirror, and I noticed a set of lights that weren't there before.

It wasn't unusual for there to be other drivers on the road, though traffic in Orchard Hollow was on the slow side. The headlights got brighter and brighter as the car behind me closed in. *Are their high beams on?*

My fingers curled tightly over the steering wheel and I started to slow down, giving the car ample room to pass me. The road we were on was narrow and only allowed for one lane in each direction, so I had to squeeze to the shoulder quite a bit.

Behind me, the car—a truck, I now realized—sped up again, though the driver didn't switch lanes to get ahead. My heart beat faster against my ribcage as the headlights flashed in the rearview mirror, obliterating my vision with their intensity until it flooded with black.

"What the..."

The sound of wheels spinning filled the air and my seatbelt slashed across my chest as the truck rammed me from behind. My neck snapped, and I groaned, knowing I probably pulled a muscle or two. Sweat licked at my skin as I held tighter onto the steering wheel and righted the Beetle before it spun out of control.

As I did, the truck delivered another hit.

I screamed so loud I blew my own ears out. Swerving to the left, I drove into the opposite lane, praying there was no oncoming traffic. Behind me, the truck accelerated and panic set in as it closed in on my bumper. I wasn't sure how much longer I could stay in control.

My hand started to reach for the phone on the passenger seat, but I pulled it back. *No distractions.* Suddenly, an idea popped into my head. I looked into the side mirror, gauging I had another ten seconds before whoever was clearly trying to run me off the road made contact.

Keeping one hand on the wheel, I rolled down the window and stuck my other hand out. Urgency thrummed through my body and I tried my hardest to use it to my advantage. As fear built up inside me, I channeled my lightning magic and imagined it hitting the trees growing on the cliff side of the road. I should have aimed it at the son of a coffee bean trying to kill me, but I couldn't go through with it. The magic I had was unpredictable and while I wanted to get away from the truck, I had no intention of hurting anyone today.

Blue sparks flooded my fingertips, and I thrust my arm further out of the window, letting go of the magic.

Flashes of lightning burst from my skin and flew across the road and into a nearby tree right ahead of me. The electric current slammed into the wood, cutting it clean across. The tree wobbled briefly, then toppled over, zooming through the air and picking up speed as it crashed down.

As it fell, I stepped on the gas, begging the Beetle not to lose steam before we were through. The car huffed and puffed, but the engine stayed strong. I drove like a maniac, making it past the falling tree just in time.

It crashed into the road behind me, taking up almost both lanes. I heard the swerve of tires as the truck driver slammed on the brakes to avoid a head-on collision with the fallen tree. My breath coming short, I glanced into the rearview to see the truck stopped in the middle of the road, headlights on.

Sweating profusely, I kept speeding all the way to Cliff Row, my pulse jack hammering the entire way. Someone tried to run me off the road.

Who?

I wished I was more collected during the attack to at least get a license plate number, but who were we kidding? I was lucky my magic actually worked like it was supposed to for once or else I'd be at the bottom of the sea right now.

As I neared Bean Me Up, I didn't stop. Instead, I circled the block a few times to make sure the creep didn't follow me. Only when I was sure it was safe did I park the car and stare out the window, waiting to regain some level of calm before going in.

I had no idea who the driver was, though there was one fact I was now absolutely clear on. What happened today had something to do with Stella's death, which could only mean one thing.

I was getting close to finding out the truth and someone out there didn't like that. Perhaps enough to kill me for it.

CHAPTER 15

That night, I dreamt of unspeakable horrors. I spent most of my sleep tossing and turning, images of fires and shadowy rooms filling my mind. When I woke up, the sheets were damp and cold beneath me and my heart rattled in my chest, making it hard to catch a breath.

Guilt ate away at me for having canceled my dinner plans with Joe. After what happened with the truck, all I wanted was to crawl into bed and stay there for eternity. If I knew I'd be riddled with nightmares, I'd have accepted takeout and a bottle of wine instead.

Padding downstairs, I was pleasantly surprised to see Stella in the kitchen when I arrived. The ghost was so close to her corporeal self, I couldn't see through her at all. As I headed for the coffee machine, Stella batted her long lashes at me.

My eyes narrowed to thin slits. "What do you want?"

"Why, good morning to you too," she said sweetly.

"Good morning," I replied, then repeated, "What do you want?"

A ghostly hand waved me off as Stella huffed out a frustrated breath. She floated to the kitchen counter, peering out of the window above the sink. From here, she looked so alive it was uncanny. "Honestly, Piper," the ghost said, "can a person not be nice without having an ulterior motive?"

"A person can. You can't," I told her.

"All right, fine!" Stella twisted around to face me, a mischievous gleam in her eye. "I wanted to let you know that it's Tuesday."

Finger lingering on the power button of the coffeemaker, I eyed her quizzically. If Stella wasn't dead, I'd have guessed she hit her head and needed a trip to the hospital to make sure she wasn't concussed. What gibberish was she on about now? Of course I knew what day of the week it was. Was there anything I was supposed to do today?

My mind reeled at the possibilities, panic setting in. Deadpanning on the ghost, I asked, "Wait, is it your birthday today?"

Did ghosts celebrate their birthdays? I thought. *Surely not.*

"Pfft!" Stella exclaimed. "A lady never reveals her birthdate."

I rubbed the bridge of my nose. "That's age. A lady never reveals her age."

"Nonsense, they're one and the same," the ghost replied. "And no, it is not, if you must know."

"Then why do I care if it's Tuesday?"

Stella's face darkened. The lines around her eyes crinkled, and she cast a gloomy glare in my direction. "Fouster is often at the casino on Tuesdays."

While Stella's eyes returned to the window, I sprinkled cinnamon on my coffee, trying to decide if I dared venture out after what happened yesterday. It was clear my familiar was determined for me to speak with her husband's business partner and I couldn't blame her. Stella's memories were few and far between, so whatever unease she felt towards Fouster and their violent interaction, I shouldn't take it lightly.

But then there was the matter of someone trying to kill me. Possibly even Fouster himself.

I considered my options as I stood between a boulder and a hard place. There really was no choice, was there?

Downing my coffee in one big gulp, I reached for the stash of breakfast bars on the counter, shoving two in my back pocket. I sighed as I waved to get Stella's attention. "Fine, you win," I told the ghost. "What's the name of the place?"

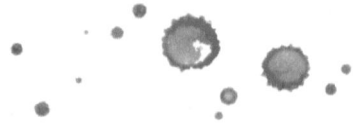

The Royal Thunder Casino stood out like a sore thumb on the horizon. Sitting on a flat stretch between the mountains, the casino looked like a commercial eyesore and one that didn't belong in Orchard Hollow. It was far enough out of town that it didn't ruin the cozy atmosphere we had going for us, but way too close for my comfort. Granted, I didn't even know about the place until I met Stella. It wasn't as though I was the type of woman who frequented casinos.

As I pulled into the huge lot, one thing caught my attention and it wasn't the three story concrete box with the casino's name boldly displayed on its roof. The parking lot was deserted.

Sure, it was early in the morning—I chose not to wait until later since I couldn't justify leaving Rory alone again—but even the trash bucket of a casino where Sam worked was busier. If I had to guess, I'd say this place wasn't what paid for the Rutherford mansion.

I parked closest to the entrance in one of the many empty spots and hurried inside. Despite the lack of clientele, the casino was a sight to be seen. If I had to describe the place, only one word came to mind: luxury.

The Royal Thunder had it in spades.

As I walked in, I was greeted by a pristine lobby area. Every inch seemed to be covered in marble and brass, and it smelled of fresh lilacs. My eyes traveled to the domed faux-ceiling and the fluffy clouds painted there. In the center of the dome, a gargantuan crystal chandelier hung down, reflecting the light across the walls. There was a seating area with several leather couches to my right and massive wooden doors with brass handles to my left.

"Welcome to the Royal Thunder," a voice boomed behind me.

I spun around to the glass-enclosed reception I had failed to notice before. Behind it, a young woman gaped at me, her gray and gold uniform sparkling clean. She waved me over, never dropping the stone-cold stare. It was unnerving.

"Will you be requiring an exchange?" she asked.

I crooked an eyebrow. "Pardon me?"

"Chips," the woman clarified. "Will you be requiring chips for the tables?"

Right. This was a casino, after all. I shook my head.

"No, thank you. I was hoping to speak to Fouster Koller. I believe he's in today."

The woman's stare faltered, and she shut her mouth tight as she inspected me. Her eyes jumped to a spot behind me, looking for what I assume was a security guard. I doubted this place got many visitors asking for the owner, so I couldn't blame her for being careful. Not that I looked like I was about to rob the joint.

Trying to put her at ease, I backed away from the counter. "I was a friend of Stella Rutherford's," I told her. "I'm hoping to ask Fouster a quick question, then I'll be out of your hair."

"Oh." Some of the concern washed away from her features. "Let me check if he's available."

Leaving me to my own devices, she picked up a phone and dialed. I couldn't make out what she said as the woman made sure to turn to the side, a security mechanism I was certain she developed working here. When she hung up and turned back toward the window, I was ready to be disappointed.

Turned out, it was my lucky day. Shockingly. "Mr. Koller can see you in five minutes," the woman said. "You're welcome to go into the main casino while you wait."

She pointed to the big wooden doors and my skin cooled. "I'll wait out here if that's all right."

The woman nodded, proceeding to return her attention to a computer screen and paying me no mind. I awkwardly drifted to the couches and the leather squeaked as I lowered to sit, my teeth gnashing together. While I waited, I pulled out my phone and dug up what I could on Fouster Koller.

The online search yielded some results, most of which detailed Koller's acquisition of the casino alongside Arthur Rutherford. It described the grand opening and when I clicked on some of the photos, it really did appear to be a popular spot. This was five years ago. As I scrolled down, I noticed the casino mentions became less prominent. That explained the lack of people here.

It was looking like the Royal Thunder had run out of steam.

"Hello?"

I jumped in my seat, the phone tumbling from my clammy fingers and slamming into the carpet below. Reaching down quickly, I pocketed it and looked up. Towering above me was the silver fox of all silver foxes. Dressed in a black turtleneck and gray trousers, the man watching me with careful, amber eyes was one of the more attractive male specimens I'd ever laid eyes on. He was likely twice my age, but that didn't seem to matter because my cheeks were on fire and my neck felt like it was blotchy with hives.

I tried to regain some composure by smiling but it came out lopsided, like a clown whose makeup dripped off under the heat of the lights. "Mr. Koller?" I asked, my voice mousy and gross. "Fouster Koller?"

"That's me," the man said. "And you are? Christine didn't mention a name when she called."

Bolstering my bravado, I uncurled my spine and stood up. Even with my shoulders pulled back, I didn't reach past Fouster's chin. "I probably should have introduced myself," I started. "My name is Piper Addison. I was a friend of Stella's."

Fouster's eyes darkened to a deep chocolate. "She did mention that, though."

"I was hoping to ask you a few quick questions," I added. "It won't take long."

Rubbing the back of his neck, the fox appeared to be incredibly uncomfortable in my presence. His gaze kept jumping around the room, always coming short of mine. If I had to bet, I'd think he was hiding something. Maybe even road rage.

I pocketed the thought, gesturing to the couch. "I promise I'll be quick, you'd really be helping me out here."

Hesitantly, Fouster walked to the opposite side of where I stood and lowered to perch on an armrest. It was probably the most uncomfortable position I could think of, and that was counting the hot yoga class Cilia made me take a few weeks ago.

"As long as this is quick," Fouster said, rearranging himself. He was now half on the couch and half on the arm rest. *Weirdo.* "You said you're a friend of Arthur's?"

"Not quite. Stella."

"Ahhh." Fouster breathed out. "From her time before."

What? I wasn't sure what he meant, but assumed he was referring to before she met Arthur. Yet the tone in his voice implied it was a time in Stella's life to be ashamed of and I instantly assumed he was referring to the same thing Sam noted; Stella's less than honest past.

Biting the inside of my cheek, I smiled as widely as my mouth would allow. "Were you two close?" I asked. Before me, Fouster's expression fermented, and I realized how incriminating my question sounded. "What I mean is, did you know her well? I've been thinking a lot about her lately and it would be nice to talk to someone who knew her."

Laying it on a little, don't you think?

Apparently, I wasn't.

"I'm not sure what Stella told you before she died, but we did not get on well," Fouster answered. "I suppose our personalities clashed."

That was one way of putting it. Stella said she remembered this man pushing her during an argument. That sounded like more than two people simply not getting along.

I steeled my racing heart. "Oh, I'm surprised," I said, feigning shock. "I thought you two would have been close, considering she was married to your business partner."

You could sense the tension in Fouster's body in the air. Energy reading was not one of my witch specialties—I had no specialties—but even I could tell the man didn't like talking about Stella. *Is it because you killed her?*

Fouster's cough interrupted my train of thought. I opened my eyes wide, staring at him intently when he said, "We had some disagreements right before the accident."

"What about?"

He shook his head, his deep-set eyes rolling skyward. "You know how it is with these things. A wife enjoys being involved in the matters of her husband. In our case, Stella was a little too involved for my liking."

It didn't surprise me that Stella stuck her nose in where it didn't belong. That woman had a knack for offering an opinion when one wasn't asked for. Was that enough to kill her over? I didn't know.

"Stella could be difficult," I admitted. "She mentioned one particular argument you two had that sounded more extreme..."

Fouster blanched. "She told you about that?" His hand was back to rubbing his neck, and I saw the faintest drop of sweat on his brow. "It was a dumb mistake. I never should have let it escalate."

I couldn't believe he was admitting it. I wanted to leap across the couch and slap the sexy son of a latte, but talked myself off the ledge before I did something idiotic.

"Look, you have to understand," Fouster continued. "Stella really got under my skin. I'm not sure how much she told you, but the casino wasn't, isn't, doing well. I was trying to talk some sense into Arthur, spitball ideas that might help us out of this mess. But Stella had to have a say and Arthur did what she told him."

"Sounds like he trusted her opinion."

Fouster sighed. "He did. Too much. The man spent more time and money pleasing that woman than he did on the business. Did you know that he actually leveraged the casino to up their life insurance policies? And don't even ask me how many times he re-mortgaged that ridiculous house they bought. But hey, what can you do? She had him wrapped around his finger."

My mind spun and my vision spotted. Stella never mentioned money trouble, and she certainly didn't tell me Arthur upped their insurance. Unless she didn't know... Was it possible Arthur took out a larger life insurance on his wife, then killed her to get out of debt? My heart jolted. I'd hate to tell Stella this. More than that, I'd hate it if I was right.

Crossing my legs, I leaned forward, my chest almost touching my thigh. Whatever I thought Arthur did, it wasn't why I came here today. "Did the argument get physical?" I asked.

"Geez, are you serious?" Fouster exclaimed, his palm slapping the couch cushion. It was such a loud reaction, I noticed the teller's eyes dart toward us from behind the glass. "Tell me she didn't say I hit her or anything similarly ridiculous."

"I'm not sure that's the word you want to use."

"Right, of course not," Fouster said. "You have to excuse me. Stella was continuously dramatic. I never hurt her, no matter what she told you. We argued, and I turned to walk away. She chased after me, probably to have the last say in the matter. I must have spun around too abruptly because I slammed right into her and she went flying back. But she was fine! We even laughed about it after." He placed an index finger at each temple. "Honestly, that woman was a handful. I have no idea how Arthur put up with her for all those years. Did she tell you about the time I had to drag her out of the casino?"

My eyes blinked rapidly. "No. What for?"

"An argument with a client I thought was going south fast. I don't know what set Stella off, but she looked like she wanted to kill the poor woman." He rubbed the rear of his neck. "That happened more often than I care to admit. Stella's anger could get the best of her, though that was probably the worst I'd seen it."

"Did she tell you who the woman was?"

Fouster shrugged. "I don't think Stella even knew her. They argued at one of the tables so I'm assuming it had to do with a game. Stella didn't like to lose."

"Um, yeah," I whispered.

Fouster's face reddened. "Sorry, I know you were friends."

I brushed him off.

"No, you're right. Stella really is...was a lot to handle. It was so shocking to hear how she died. I guess I was trying to make sense of her life. To find some sort of explanation for what happened."

"I'm sorry I can't offer you one," Fouster said. "If it helps, I wish I was more patient with her while she was alive."

I didn't want to admit it, but his sentiment did help. Somehow, I believed he meant it. If anyone knew how infuriating Stella could be, it was me, so I couldn't very well fault Fouster for getting fed up with her. There were plenty of times I wanted to strangle the bossy woman myself.

I started to stand, then paused. "Any chance you remember where you were that night? When Stella had her accident."

"Here," Fouster answered. "Arthur and I were going over business plans. I actually managed to get him to consider my ideas if you can believe it. He left around eleven, but I stayed behind. I usually stay quite late. Why do you ask?"

I blushed. "No reason. Thank you for speaking with me."

As I turned to leave, Fouster looped around me and said, "I'm sorry about your friend. If you ever need someone to talk to, give me a call."

His hand reached for mine and I felt the rough edge of a piece of paper in my palm. I looked down, my jaw unhinging as I stared at Fouster's business card with his cell phone number etched on the front. Was this guy hitting on me? And while I was clearly distraught over the death of my friend?

I was starting to see why Stella may have disliked him. Attractive or not, that was a tasteless move.

Rushing out of the casino, I was halfway to my car when my phone vibrated. I pulled it out, confused. It was the security alarm for Bean Me Up. Someone must have tripped it while I was here.

I checked the time, frowning. *Rory.*

As I drove away from the casino, I replayed my conversation with Fouster. My mind was full of his words and everything they helped explain. Nerves ate away at me as I thought about calling Romero to tell him his hunch about Arthur Rutherford may have been correct. Stella would never forgive me.

Perhaps if I could actually prove her husband wasn't the loving man she thought he was, she might come around.

Though knowing Stella, probably not.

My head was swimming when I pulled up next to the cafe and walked out. As I neared the door, the hairs on my arms stood up and I froze in my tracks.

The glass on the front door was shattered. It lay in a sparkling mess on the tile floor, the open sign that usually hung on it lying off to the side. My chest constricted and my toes danced inside my boots as I carefully stepped inside Bean Me Up.

My beautiful cafe was in shambles. The tables were overturned, the espresso machine had a massive gash down the side, even the spaceship clock lay smashed on the floor.

Who would do this?

I yipped towards the register, finding it secure and locked. It wasn't a robbery. Then what would—

The keys dropped from my hand and crashed to the ground. Unable to move, I stared at the wall opposite me in silence, my lips sounding out the words painted in bright red paint on the wallpaper.

"Back off or else."

CHAPTER 16

S team billowed from the spout of the kettle, fogging up the kitchen counter. As I chewed my nails down to the bone, Joe walked over to turn it off, pouring the hot water into two mugs sitting beside the stove. My eyes fought to focus on the roaring fire before me. I'd been camped out on the couch in the farmhouse since Joe drove me home earlier today.

By the time one of the deputies Romero sent to the cafe finished questioning me, I was too exhausted to drive. My brain was mush and my body felt like someone dropped a piano on me; broken and liquid.

I called Joe as soon as some of my senses returned and he came immediately. Even closed the bookshop for the day to help me break the news to Rory that Bean Me Up was out of commission again. My head hurt thinking about it. How many times was my precious baby going to be shut down? I felt like the worst business mom ever.

A hot mug of tea slid across the coffee table toward me as Joe settled into the couch cushions. "Black with two sugars," he said, pushing the mug closer. "Let me know when you're hungry and I'll whip something up."

Whip something up? I didn't even know Joe knew how to cook. Not because I assumed the worst, but being a vampire, he had no need for human sustenance. It would make sense he didn't learn the skill.

Reading my mind, Joe said, "It helps keep up appearances, and I actually enjoy cooking."

"That makes sense," I said, blowing on the tea.

Joe was one of the paranormals who was hush-hush about his magical abilities, as most vampires were. Unlike warlocks and witches, the vampires and werewolves kept their magic to themselves. It stood to reason they'd do so, considering theirs was the type of magic humans feared the most. Funnily enough, a warlock's brand of magic could do more damage than that of a vampire and yet the blood-suckers got the bad reputation. Humans were odd that way.

I brought the mug to my lips but didn't drink. "I can't believe this is happening again."

"At least no one died this time," Joe said, lightening the mood.

I laughed, but my mood didn't feel any brighter.

"It might be best if you kept the cafe closed for a bit," Joe said. "Until Romero's team can find out who's responsible for the vandalism."

"I know who's responsible. The same person who chased me in the truck," I said.

After today, I ended up telling Joe about the earlier incident and he was less than impressed with my keeping it to myself. In my defense, I didn't want to worry him until I had more information. And I certainly didn't want to tell Romero about it since he'd likely ask me to step away from Stella's case.

I wasn't ready to do that yet.

Beside me, Joe shifted his weight uncomfortably. "That brings me to my next point," he said. "I think you should stop looking into Stella's death. For now."

Setting the tea down, I watched the steam rise from the top and disperse into the air. My tired eyes half-shut as my thoughts clouded my foggy mind. I pressed the pads of my palms to my eyes and rubbed them. "I can't stop now," I told Joe. "I'm getting close to the truth."

"Too close," he said. His hand reached for my arm

and pulled it away from my face, then snaked around my shoulder. As he pulled me in, my shoulders relaxed and I settled into his chest, taking slow, deliberate breaths. "I'm worried that if you keep pushing, whoever is sending you these messages will escalate. You're going to get yourself into a serious situation if you don't stop."

"I know but—"

Joe groaned, and I sealed my lips. He was right, of course. In the span of two days, I was almost driven off a cliff and had my business destroyed. Whoever was behind this was clearly watching me, and while that should have scared me into hiding, it seemed to do the exact opposite. I wanted to keep going.

But that was dumb. I had to listen to Joe and back off before I went the way Stella did.

As if on cue, cold air pummeled my face as Stella Rutherford flung into the room. Her hair, usually up in a shiny ponytail, looked mussed and for a second, I thought I noticed a few grays sticking out. It was hard to tell considering her lackluster ghostly appearance. She glanced at Joe and I cuddling on the couch with one eyebrow quirked.

"I'm glad the threats to your life are having a positive effect on your libido," Stella sniped.

I bristled, pushing away from Joe to sit up straight.

"Hello to you too, Stella," I said. "Can I remind you that you're the reason all this is happening?"

"I beg to differ."

"Are you kidding? You basically pushed me in Fouster's direction!"

The ghost's jaw dropped open. "You think Fouster did this?" she asked, her head shaking.

"Not exactly," I said sheepishly. I was yet to tell Stella I was leaning in Arthur's direction again. "But it is all too coincidental that someone came for me right after you remembered the fight you had. Which he explained, by the way."

Stella scoffed. "As he would. Don't let that man fool you. He is no angel."

Quickly relaying what the ghost said to Joe, I leaned forward, reaching for the tea again. I wished there was a way to make Joe see my familiar. Constantly having to repeat what was being said was becoming exhausting. When I finished talking, I turned my focus back to the ghost. "What do you mean about Fouster? Did you remember anything else?"

"Not exactly," she replied. "After you told me what he said about the casino, I started thinking. Fouster and I never got along, but I would never stand in the way of Arthur's business. Unless..."

Her blue eyes burnt into me.

"Unless what he was suggesting wasn't legal," I guessed. "Why would you think that?"

"Before the two partnered up, Fouster had a rep when it came to his previous ventures. Two of his businesses went up in flames a few years apart. As far as I know, both were accidents, but Fouster sure cleaned up because of them. Arthur said I was being suspicious for no reason, and maybe I was. The guy wasn't clean cut, I knew it, but I couldn't prove it."

My spine steeled. "Did you try to prove it?"

"Regretfully, no," Stella said. "Arthur would never go into business with a crook, not after he paid his dues for the money laundering. I trusted his judgment and let it go."

"But you never saw eye to eye with Fouster."

Stella nodded and my heart dropped into my stomach. All this talk about illegal activity and casinos reminded me that I was yet to ask her about her past. One that she conveniently hadn't mentioned when she sent me off to talk to Fouster. I wasn't sure if Stella's past had anything to do with how she died, but she sure was throwing some stones in her glass house.

Thinking of Stella's life before she was a Rutherford made my mind instantly jump to Arthur and the insurance policy Fouster mentioned. The balls rolled in my brain, words swimming around as I grabbed on to each one until something clicked. Insurance. Fraud. Casino. Could there be anything there?

I dug into my jean pocket and pulled out my cell phone, facing Joe. "How much do you know about insurance fraud?"

"I'm sorry, why?"

I started to type, my attention drifting. "A hunch. Stella is convinced Fouster had less than legal ideas for the casino. When I was there, I noticed the place was empty. It was strange. Even if the business wasn't doing well, as Fouster suggested, I'd expect there to be more activity in a facility that size. A cleaning crew, a security guard, someone else, you know? When I came in, it was only the teller and Fouster."

Joe shrugged. "Too early in the day, perhaps?"

"It's possible. Or there could be a more sinister reason." My fingers typed speedily, and I brought the phone to my face, reading. "The fires were in the paper," I said, turning the screen around.

He grabbed it from my hands. "Is this right? It says here Fouster came out with over a million for each location that burned down."

Eyes flicking to Stella, I waited until she nodded to confirm, then let out a low whistle. "No wonder you didn't want to hear any of his ideas," I told the ghost. "I bet you they involved matches and a whole lot of gasoline."

They might still, I thought, keeping it to myself. Sure, there was a chance Fouster was planning to burn down the casino for insurance money or it could be what Joe said; I may have visited on a slow day. Either way, I should let Romero know what I discovered so he could keep an eye on the guy before he set the entire town ablaze accidentally.

Before I could follow through, Stella shrieked and my eardrums exploded. I spun around, following her panicked stare to the fireplace. Hanging off the edge of the mantel was Harry Houdini, his bushy tail dangerously close to the rising flames. Reaching out, I smacked Joe on the arm and we both shot up to rush toward the beast. Behind me, Stella screamed again, and I wondered if she was actually starting to enjoy Harry's company. Then I realized she was telling us to let karma do her work. Flashing her an angry glare, I jumped over the coffee table and leapt for the raccoon.

Lucky for the troublemaker, Joe beat me to it and caught Harry by the scruff of the neck before he could plummet into the fire. He tsked, placing the raccoon on the floor where he immediately hissed and ran off.

My breath caught in my paper-thin lungs. "He is getting worse and worse," I said.

"It seems Harry's need for snacks outweighs his survival instinct," Joe noted, pointing to the half open bag of cookies on the mantel. "Might want to lock these up."

As he tossed me the bag, I considered Harry's foolish bravery. Nothing stood between the rascal and what he wanted. No amount of danger was going to deter him. I could learn a thing or two from Harry Houdini. My eyes flew to Stella hovering in the corner of the room with a dazed look on her face and I knew what I had to do. No matter what dangers were stacking up against me, I needed to keep digging. I owed it to my familiar to uncover the truth.

Dusting off invisible dirt from my pants, I walked to the kitchen to hide the cookies, a list forming in my head.

Step one, fill Romero in on everything I discovered thus far. Step two, change the locks at Bean Me Up and get it up and running again. Step three, the one I least looked forward to, go back to the Rutherford estate. Between the life insurance Arthur took out, his previous illegal dealings, and Fouster's sketchy background, someone was lying.

The only issue was, I wasn't sure which of the two men in Stella's life was the bigger deceiver.

CHAPTER 17

The ghost was fuming. Literally.

I tried not to laugh as Stella crossed her arms, nostrils flaring; her anger so vivid it billowed around her like smoke. There was only one other instance my familiar's incorporeal shape took on this strange form, and I was certain this was worse than the time Harry Houdini peed through her leg. The ghost's face twisted in disgust. "You and me, we're done!"

"You're really exaggerating," I said, my eyes rolling. "Did you not hear what I said? He upped your life insurance right before you bit the bullet."

The smoke around her intensified as Stella slapped her arms against her side for emphasis. "After all the things I did for you, this is how you repay me?" she roared. "I turn myself inside out to help you better yourself and instead of thanking me, you're accusing my husband of what? Killing me for money? Arthur doesn't need more money, Piper. He has plenty."

"First," I raised a finger, "I never asked you for life advice. And second, I am not saying he killed you. All I'm saying is I want to have a little chat to see if anything Fouster said is true. Aren't you the least bit curious?"

Biting her bottom lip, Stella uncurled her fisted palms. She stomped across the room, making sure to land her feet, instead of float, for emphasis. Her tennis skirt swayed from side to side behind her as her long legs strode to the door.

Great, now she was leaving.

I had no time to chase after an angry ghost. When I called Arthur and he reluctantly agreed to meet me at his casino, he made sure I knew he couldn't spare a minute longer than was necessary. Either he was over my questions, or he heard about me following his daughter. Hopefully, it wasn't the latter. From what Stella told me, he was extremely protective of the kid.

Pulling on a light camel trench coat, I grabbed the keys from the console table, pulled on my boots, and hiked it out the door. My heart gave a jolt, noting the time. On any other day, I'd be heading into work right now.

I slid into the driver's seat, my mouth downturned.

"You better not upset him."

A scream expelled from me. I slammed my palms into the steering wheel and twisted around to see Stella perching on the edge of the backseat. Her expression and the temperature inside the Beetle were equally frosty.

"Stella! Stop scaring me!"

My familiar deadpanned at me, then glanced at the torn leather she sat on. "The only scary thing in here is the monstrosity you call a vehicle."

I sucked in a breath and spun around, rubbing the dashboard gently.

"Don't worry," I whispered to the car, "she didn't mean it."

"I did. Especially the part about Arthur. He can't handle stress at his age."

Shaking my head, I started the engine and cringed as it sputtered to life. In the rearview mirror, Stella smirked. She was on my last nerve this morning. Honestly, if the woman wasn't already dead, I'd consider strangling her myself.

Meeting her eyes in the mirror, I waited for the heat to kick in, then said, "If I promise to be nice, will you leave me alone, please?"

"Absolutely not," Stella announced. "I'm coming with you." Before I could object, she crossed her arms and gaped out the window, adding, "You might want to speed it up, if this bucket on wheels can move faster than a tortoise on valium."

Stella spent the entire ride to the Royal Thunder Casino in the backseat like I was a car service she'd hired. Occasionally, she cast me dreary glances in the mirror, but for the most part, the ghost remained fixated on the sea as we drove. Her finger played with a diamond earring large enough to double as a paper weight.

I stayed quiet too. It was nice not to hear her complain for once.

When we finally arrived and I parked, my familiar's body grew rigid. Her shoulders jutted out more than they usually did and her back stayed ramrod straight, pressed against the car seat. As I opened the door, Stella's body blinked out of sight.

"See you inside, I guess," I mumbled, making my way into the casino.

The place was as empty as it was the first time I visited. No shock there. Actually, it felt even more abandoned today, and I briefly panicked, thinking Fouster might burn it down with me in it. My worry was short-lived because before I could hyperventilate into my sleeve and run back to the car, the same teller greeted me from behind her glass cage.

"Mr. Rutherford will see you in his office," she said, gesturing to a door off to the side I didn't notice before. "He asked me to remind you that he must leave at exactly ten."

I nodded, glancing at the vintage watch Gran gave me. I had exactly fifteen minutes to get my answers. Not a lot of time, but I'd worked with less. I nearly laughed at myself. Who died and made me a detective?

My stomach tightened. Stella, that's who.

Nodding at the teller, I slinked around the wall of glass and hurried through the door. My eyes squinted as a bright light filled the narrow hallway as I walked, the atmosphere here a polar opposite to the lobby. Where the lobby was luxurious and inviting, this area of the casino felt sterile and bland. Bright white walls, fluorescent boxes on the ceiling, and metal doors along both sides. It was what I imagined being inside a spaceship was like.

Walking slowly, I read the brass labels on each door I passed. My gait slowed further at the sight of Fouster Koller's office until I was idling next to it. Ears perked, I tried to listen for sounds on the other side of the door, but either Fouster wasn't in, or he was dead quiet.

Another door opened to my left, and I jumped to attention, continuing to walk so I wasn't caught spying on the casino owner red-handed.

"Miss Addison." Arthur's familiar low tone floated toward me. "Come on in."

Stella's husband stepped aside, motioning to the office he stood next to. Today, he wore a similar expensive suit as last time, except this one was a deep burgundy. I had to hand it to Arthur Rutherford; the man knew how to dress. Not that it surprised me, considering he was married to Stella.

As I walked inside, I realized we weren't alone.

"Don't look so aghast," Stella said. Her legs crossed as she reclined in the chair opposite the only window in the room, positioning herself at end of the large mahogany desk in the center of the office.

I didn't reply, acknowledging her only with the tip of my chin. While Stella gazed lovingly at Arthur, who was settling into a lofty leather chair near the window, I inspected his office. It was incredibly furnished with mid-century modern pieces combined with several contemporary choices. In the corner of the room stood a fluid sculpture made entirely of metal, beside it a round, wood side table cozied up to an Eames lounger. Opposite them was the desk we sat at, adorned with only the necessities. A laptop, a monogrammed agenda, and a gold pen I was sure cost more than my car.

My eyes slid to the single floating shelf behind Arthur and I examined the few photographs on it. One of Nicki on a large yacht, her hair flowing behind her in the wind. Another of her at what appeared to be a charity event. And the last frame, the one that caught my eye the most. It was a photo of the three of them, Arthur, Nicki, and Stella, settled in on a white sofa. From the look of the background, I guessed it was taken in their home and by Stella's overly done face, I'd wager not long before she died.

Arthur tapped the gold pen against the desk, jarring me. "I don't mean to rush you, but as I mentioned earlier, I have a meeting this morning."

"Yes, right," I said. "I'll get to the point."

Next to me, Stella mumbled, "Please do."

I dutifully ignored her.

"I'm not sure if he mentioned it, but I was here earlier in the week to speak with Mr. Koller."

Arthur's gray eyebrows hiked. "He didn't say," he replied. "Though we haven't spoken much. You know how it is with a business this large."

I nodded, even though I had no idea how it was at all. Shifting uncomfortably in the chair, I worked to keep eye contact with Stella's husband. "I'm going to come right out and say it. Fouster said you took out a large life insurance policy on Stella not long before she died."

"I honestly can't believe you," Stella whispered.

I waved her off under the table. "I'm not insinuating anything," I said quickly. "Though you must admit it looks suspicious."

Before me, the man's forehead crinkled as he pushed off the chair and stood. His gaze jumped to the empty seat beside me and for a second I wondered if he could see Stella there, or at least feel her. As briefly as it happened, Arthur's eyes left the chair and his wife's ghost and landed on the photographs sitting atop the shelf. He picked up the one of all three Rutherfords, examining it closely.

"After it happened," Arthur said, "the police wouldn't leave that part alone either. Not that I blame them. The business was going under and I don't exactly have the cleanest of slates."

I didn't know what to say, so I stayed quiet. Surprisingly, so did Stella.

"For a few weeks before her accident, Stella was acting strangely. I didn't mention it before because I didn't want you dragging her name through the mud, but you seem to be good at drawing out information, so there's no point hiding things." He cast me a knowing glance. I blushed, realizing he was referring to my conversation with Nicki. "I truly thought it was our dire financial situation getting to her, which is exactly what I told the police. I knew how it appeared once they started nosing about in our insurance."

Throat dry, I cleared it twice before speaking. "Did Stella mention a fight she had with Fouster? One that got out of hand?"

"No," Arthur replied, his head shaking. "But those two were constantly in disagreement. I don't know what you've been able to gather in your search; but you should know Fouster has the same troubled past as me when it comes to money."

"I may have figured that out already."

Stella scoffed. My eyes darted sideways, a silent "hush" lingering on my lips.

"Yes, well, unlike me," Arthur explained, placing the frame on the table, "Fouster has less self-control. He was pressuring me to get involved in some unsavory tactics to recoup our investment, tactics I wanted nothing to do with."

"I knew it!" Stella yelped.

Jolting, I recovered my shock from her yelling by leaning forward on the desk to look at the photograph closer. "Did Stella know about this?"

"She did, yes. To be honest, I thought it was the reason she was acting oddly. Then she asked me to up her life policy."

Both Stella and I did a double take. My jaw hit the

top of the desk and next to me, the ghost was speech-less for the first time in her life and afterlife.

I rubbed my chin. "Are you saying it wasn't your decision?"

"Of course not!" Arthur exclaimed. "I had no reason to think of it." His skin went white as bone as he looked around the room, seemingly checking that we were alone. "Look, I never told the police this, but after Stella died, I had a theory. What if she did it to help us? To keep me and Nicki financially secure?"

My focus drifted to the ghost, and I eyed her questioningly. Stella shrugged in return. I could tell immediately by the surprised look on her face she was as out of the loop with the discovery as I was. I wanted to ask Arthur to explain further when an object in the photo on the desk caught my eye.

I reached for it, raising the frame up to my face. "Did Stella wear this bracelet often?" I asked, motioning to the gaudy, diamond-encrusted chain around her wrist.

"She never left the house without it," Arthur answered. "Come to think of it, I don't recall seeing it since the accident. I should call the police to ask."

"You really should. It looks like it's worth a lot."

This finally got Stella talking. "It is!" the ghost exclaimed. "I completely forgot about it, but Arthur is right, I always had it on."

She looked down at her empty wrist.

Acid swirled inside me as realization settled in. If Stella died with the bracelet on, her ghost would be wearing it. Nothing else changed in her outfit from the way she was dressed the day it happened. Even those atrocious diamond earrings remained in her ears. Then why was the bracelet gone?

I thought back to Romero's description of the crime scene and swallowed thickly. *The bruise on her wrist when they found her. It could have been caused by a large chain being ripped off.*

My lips parted, then shut as the office door swung open behind us. I twisted around in the chair, my knees knocking.

"Piper!" Fouster yelled, his close proximity to me implying we were closer than we were. *Slimeball.* "I thought I heard your voice."

Teeth chattering, I tried not to think about what else he overheard. "Nice to see you again, Mr. Koller."

Calling him by his last name had the exact effect I was going for. Fouster cringed, his jaw working as he tried to appear nonchalant.

"She shoots," Stella whispered, "she scores."

As the ghost continued to glower, Fouster crossed the room and placed a tablet on the desk to face me. He smiled cockily; I rolled my eyes when he wasn't looking. I leaned into the screen, realizing I was looking at a frozen video frame of a casino.

"Is that—"

"Security footage from the main floor," Fouster said. Then, looking at Arthur, "I'll explain later."

He shifted the tablet to place it in my direct sight-line and pressed the play button. "I was able to find footage of the night we discussed. The argument Stella had with the customer. I thought you might want to see it."

"It can't hurt to check it out," I said gratefully.

As the black and white footage played, I attempted to make out what was happening. There were two women standing next to a poker table having a heated discussion. One of them was definitely Stella and the other woman I couldn't place. She had short black hair, but the vantage point made it impossible to see her face. I squinted as a tall security guard approached the two. After a minute of talking, the second woman was escorted out and Stella stalked away in a huff, off camera.

"Were you able to find out who the woman was?" I asked Fouster.

He nodded. "Security records indicated it was someone by the name of Catherine Strand. Not sure if that means anything to you."

Slouching, I let go of a defeated sigh. The name didn't ring a bell at all. Another dead end. Wonderful.

"Catherine Strand my tight behind!" Stella announced from behind me.

I swiveled around, her cold transparent skin an inch from mine. The ghost's gaze was locked on the tablet and her brows kissed as she pointed a slender finger at the screen.

"That isn't any Catherine," Stella hissed out. "That's Valerie. I'd bet my life on it."

My mind clung to her announcement, the pieces falling together. It seemed that Valerie didn't disappear after all. But what was she doing in Orchard Hollow? And what did Stella and her argue about? As soon as I left here today, I planned to stop by the police station and ask the sheriff to look into the fake name Valerie used. We might get lucky.

Stella's last words flashed before me. "I'd bet my life on it."

Terror gripped every bone in my body as I regarded my familiar. Maybe she did.

CHAPTER 18

My back ached as I bent down to pick up another large shard of glass and tossed it into the trash can at my feet. Eyes watering, I worked to keep my emotions at bay while cleaning up Bean Me Up. It was not working. Since coming here after my visit to the casino, I had already cried three times, ate two scones back-to-back, and downed four coffees. To make matters worse, whoever vandalized the place did a number on the espresso machine so I had to settle for drip coffee instead of the apple spiced latte I desperately craved.

Lounging on the counter with her legs crossed and her back arched was Stella. She watched me with a narrow-eyed expression like a lion stalking its prey.

"Can you please just say something already?" I groaned, tossing the last of the broken flower vases into the trash. "I didn't accuse anyone of anything, so I'm not sure why you're upset with me this time."

Stella vanished as soon as she revealed Valerie's identity on the security footage and hadn't spoken a word since she reappeared at the cafe a half hour after I got in. As fantastic as it was to have some peace and quiet for a change, I was beginning to worry. The ghost's memory was slowly trickling in and I had the distinct feeling it was driving her mad.

Perched on the countertop, Stella brought the tips of her hair to her face, inspecting them for split ends. "Why did she lie?"

I tied off the bag in the bin and dragged it over to the others stacked by the office door. Wiping the sweat off my brow, I picked up a rag and began to wipe down all the surfaces. It was surprising how much I accomplished in the last hour, but it didn't matter; it would be a while until I could reopen the cafe to the public. No way was I subjecting Rory and myself to another possible attack.

That was what I should have been thinking about as I cleaned. Except it wasn't. My mind was locked on Stella's question. Why *did* Valerie lie about her name?

"The guy at Christopher's apartment said they dropped off the face of the earth," I told Stella, aimlessly rubbing the cloth across the marble top. "Maybe they ran away for a reason. Money issues perhaps?"

"Valerie was never one to run away from her problems," my familiar argued. "Besides, I knew her real identity. Lying to security about her name simply doesn't add up."

She wasn't wrong. The more I thought about the video I saw at the casino, the less it made sense. If Valerie wanted to stay off the radar, why bother seeking Stella out? I wished the ghost would hurry up and get her memory back because all our answers were locked inside her dead noggin and there was no coaxing them out.

Tossing the rag into the sink behind me, I padded to the back office, returning with my laptop. With Stella deep in thought, I focused on finding whatever I could on Catherine Strand. The first search yielded no results. It turned out there were a surprising amount of women by that name; it took forever to get through a portion of the profiles online, none of which matched Valerie's description. Frustrated, I closed the lid and sighed audibly.

"You won't find anything," Stella said, not looking at me. "She's using a fake name for a reason. Whatever Valerie is hiding from, she won't make it easy for you to track her down. She was always clever."

I fidgeted with an empty cup on the counter. "Were you friends for long?"

"Uh-huh. Since high school."

"What happened to you two?"

A darkness gathered behind Stella's eyes as she thought about my question. She rolled her shoulders and bit her lip. "Life, I suppose," she said. "We were inseparable for a while, even after she got together with Chris."

"You really couldn't stand him, huh?"

Stella shook her head. "I thought Valerie could do better, but she didn't see herself the way I did." She brushed down her ponytail to remove non-existent frizz. "Valerie didn't come from the best place, neither of us did. It was likely why we got along so well. When Chris showed up talking a big game, she fell for it. I couldn't blame her, really. As long as she was happy, that was all that mattered."

"It sounds like what you two had was special," I mused. "Strange you stopped speaking."

"Perhaps," Stella whispered. "People change. They drift apart."

I didn't say it, but I had the feeling Stella marrying into the Rutherford family had a lot to do with the implosion of their friendship. From what she told me about Valerie, she didn't strike me as the type of woman that would fit into Stella's privileged lifestyle.

Yet to lose such a long-standing friend...it must have hurt.

"Try searching for Christopher again," Stella suggested. Her chin dipped toward the closed laptop and her jaw tensed; it was as if she could tell I was feeling sorry for her and wanted me to stop immediately.

I wished to tell her I tried that when we were in King City and didn't find a thing, but chose to avoid the argument. When the same results popped up, I turned the screen to face her and said, "Nothing here. At least nothing to tell us where he might be."

"Try the east coast," Stella instructed.

My forehead scrunched, confused.

"That's where Chris said he was from," the ghost clarified. "He could have been lying. The man had a silver tongue, but you might get lucky."

As I typed, I tried to keep one eye on my familiar. Her mood had changed drastically since the visit to the casino. It may have been that seeing Arthur again triggered her somehow, but I was willing to bet Valerie had more to do with it.

I hadn't realized how much Stella lost in her life, and that wasn't even counting the memories we were yet to uncover.

On the screen, Christopher's name caught my eye. I clicked on the article, my mouth gaping. "Holy coffee bean," I whispered. "You're not going to believe this."

"What?" Stella's neck stretched to see what I was reading.

Tilting the screen, I ran my eyes over the post, my heart racing with each word. "It says here there was a casino robbery in Petersburg and a security guard died." I skimmed the rest of the article. "According to this newspaper, he was run over chasing the robber's getaway car. He died in the hospital a few days later."

"You found this looking for Chris?"

I was as surprised as her. So far, there was nothing in the article that pointed to Valerie's boyfriend. The guard's name wasn't mentioned and I couldn't spot Christopher's name anywhere. Pulling up a fresh tab, I searched for the incident mentioned, typing in an approximate date; ten years ago tomorrow.

"Bingo!" I yelped. Clicking maniacally to read the next post, I nearly choked on my saliva when I pulled it up. "This can't be right."

"Can you please stop the theatrics and tell me what it says? Unless you're auditioning for Broadway, the drama is unnecessary."

I rolled my eyes at Stella, saying, "There were two suspects in the case."

"Let me guess," the ghost quipped. "Chris?"

"Yes. And an unidentified woman."

At that, Stella's face turned into a grayer shade of gray. Her chest rose up and down and for a second I thought I saw a bead of sweat roll down her brow. Which was, of course, impossible. "Valerie wouldn't..."

"Unless she did," I countered. "You said it yourself, Christopher had a way of getting to her. Could he have convinced her to go along with it and things got out of hand. The casino was a small one. They probably didn't think it would be that difficult."

When Stella said nothing, I checked the other related articles. There was more of the same; details of the crime, Christopher's involvement, some information on how much was stolen. Not enough to be worth a life in my opinion, but then I wasn't a casino thief. I clicked on another link, my body shuddering, when a picture of the victim popped on screen.

The security guard who died during the incident was younger than I expected. I followed his name, relieved when I found out he didn't have children. There was an obituary listing his life achievements and information on burial arrangements, including the name and contact information of his widow.

My gaze flicked to my phone. *I can't.*

Slowly, my fingers inched toward the phone and before I knew it, I was dialing the number. The line rang once, twice, three times. A light, female voice sounded and I jumped, startled. Across from me,

Stella quirked a brow. I held up a finger, listening for the security guard's widow to finish reciting her voice-mail message.

"Um, hi," I said after the beep. "I'm sorry to bother you. My name is Piper, and I was hoping to speak to you about your husband. This is going to sound strange, but I think it might be connected to my friend's death."

Leaving my number, I hung up and looked at Stella.

"Now what?" the ghost asked.

"Now we wait."

We didn't have to wait long. Within seconds, my phone vibrated in my hands. I looked at the number, deflating when I saw it wasn't the same one I dialed earlier. Pressing the phone to my ear, I waved Stella off and said, "Hello?"

"Piper?" a gruff, oddly familiar voice asked. "Piper Addison?"

I racked my brain trying to place the man on the other line. "That's me."

"It's Sam," the man answered. "From the casino."

"Sam, of course. How are you?"

Attempting my best to avoid Stella's whisper-yells, I twisted around to face the wall and kept my voice low. "I'm a little surprised to get your call. If this is about what happened to Stella, I still don't have anything to share, I'm afraid."

"It isn't," Sam said quickly. "At least not directly."

"Oh?"

There was the sound of a chair scraping against tile, followed by a door closing. I assumed Sam was at work and pictured him scurrying across the tiny office he worked out of to close the door. Intrigue worked its way up my body.

"I told you'd I'd keep an eye out," he said. "I have friends on the force. Comes with the job. After you left, I asked them to look into anything that might be related and call me if anything pops up on Stella or someone she may have known while she was here."

Adrenaline carved up my spine. "They got something on her death?" It didn't make any sense to me why cops in King City would have information on an accident that happened here in town, but I wasn't about to argue. Help was help, and I sure needed a ton of it. "That's fantastic news."

"I'm afraid this isn't a good news type of call," Sam said, his voice husky and low. "Valerie's boyfriend, Christopher, was found dead last week."

CHAPTER 19

"Dead? How?" My voice pitched as I all but screamed into the phone. Behind me, Stella made a snide remark about the glass breaking. I didn't even bother telling her off. All my attention was on Sam. Well, on dead Christopher. "Sorry for all the questions. This is very unusual timing."

"Not if you knew Christopher," Sam said.

It was beginning to look like I didn't know anything at all. What were the chances that the one clue I was trying to follow would be a literal dead end?

"If it helps, it sounds like a case of wrong place, wrong time," Sam said.

I wasn't sure how that was supposed to help. "What happened to him, exactly?"

Biting my nails, I twirled in the chair again. As I did, Stella's face popped up before me, her eyes rounded with worry. She mouthed, "what happened?" and I had to shoo her off so I could concentrate on the call. Aggravated, the ghost vibrated, then vanished. She left her anxiety behind to keep me company.

"I don't have a lot of the details, but it looks like a mugging that went south," Sam said. "Though to be honest, Christopher gravitated toward the wrong crowds, so it wouldn't surprise me to hear there was more to the story."

A chill ran through the air and the loose strands of my braid blew away as Stella returned. I put up my palm, hoping she understood that I would fill her in as soon as I got off the phone. My familiar slumped, her frustration evident.

Returning my focus to the phone, I asked, "Where was Valerie when it happened?"

"No one knows," Sam replied. "She remains in the wind. That woman sure knows how to stay hidden when she wants to."

No kidding.

Valerie was more illustrious than Stella's memories at this point. I bit the inside of my cheek, scowling. "Well, thank you for letting me know," I told Sam. "If you hear anything else, give me a call and I'll do the same."

"Actually, all this talk about Stella has me reminiscing," Sam said. His voice lowered, a slight shake at the end of his words. "I was thinking of driving down your way to visit her grave. Pay my respects, have some closure. I never got to attend the funeral and I have to admit, I feel awful about it. Would you be interested in grabbing a coffee while I'm there?"

Before me, Stella drifted closer as if she could hear what Sam said and was propelled to follow the gossip. I wondered if the ghost was as over her ex as she pretended to be. She'd been in a tizzy since Sam called.

Taking a purposeful step backward, I grinned cockily. "A coffee sounds great," I said. "I'd invite you to stop by my cafe but we've had a bit of a setback recently. When do you think you'll be by?"

"This afternoon, if you've got some time to spare, then."

With the cafe closed, I had all the time in the world. "Meet me in the Coral Reef around three."

Having agreed on a time, I hung up the phone and stayed quiet. At my silence, Stella's cheeks puffed out, and she cast me a glare that would have made any sane person run away. I, however, was used to her drama queen behavior and found the entire spectacle hilarious. Stella was definitely not over Sam. Geez, even their names sounded like they belonged together.

"Someone has it bad," I teased her.

"Piper, please. I am a married woman."

I didn't have the heart to break it to her that the vows were void since death quite literally parted her and Arthur. "Come on," I told her. "Put your newfound ghost abilities to good use and help me finish cleaning this place. I'll tell you all about the phone call while we work."

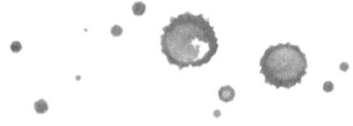

Three o'clock at the Coral Reef was busier than an emergency room on a Saturday night. I squeezed between two groups waiting for tables while the hostess marked off names on a growing list. I didn't even realize this place had someone manning the door. The last time I was here, I waltzed right in.

Perhaps it was better to cancel.

A finger tapped my shoulder as I dug at the bottomless pit that was my purse. "I got us a table near the register."

I turned slowly, Sam's familiar voice at my back. When I finally faced him, I had to stifle my frustration.

Stella was hovering so close behind the man, she was basically breathing down his neck. There was no way to shoo her off without appearing unhinged, though I did briefly consider zapping her with my magic. If there weren't so many humans around—Sam, included —I might have actually gone through with it.

"Hi, again," I said. "I'm surprised you were able to get a spot."

The security guard gestured to the belly of the restaurant. "I got here right before the rush."

"It's honestly not usually this busy. I'm not sure what's going on today."

As we walked past tables full of loud customers, Sam glanced at me over his shoulder. "They likely all came here when they saw your cafe was closed."

I chuckled. If only I were this popular.

Sam pointed to a small two-seater right next to the counter holding a modern cash system. It was on the opposite side from the kitchen and while it was fairly loud back here, at least we didn't have to listen to the cook yell out orders. I settled into the chair and scanned the restaurant for signs of Nicki. She wasn't anywhere in sight. A small victory for once.

"Ask him what he thought of the mausoleum," Stella instructed.

I would do no such thing. Not only was it obnoxious as hell that my familiar was buried in a mausoleum bigger than my house, but I wasn't about to steer the conversation that way. Sam was already dealing with a lot being here; I didn't need to add to the man's emotional stress by bringing up his ex-fiancée's death right off the bat.

Instead of following her cue, I picked up the menu and pretended to peruse the selection. All I really wanted was a good cup of coffee. A privilege I doubted the Coral Reef would have.

"So," Sam said, his thick finger flicking the corner of the laminated menu, "what's good here?"

I squirmed in my seat. "Um, I don't eat here very often. We can start with coffee?"

"Sounds great. I could use another cup."

A few minutes later, a server about Rory's age took our order and hurried to another table. I worked to keep my attention on Sam despite my nosy familiar floating around us. Each time she passed him, Sam rubbed his arms, the chill of her ghostly presence evident on his goosebump-covered skin.

"Do they have the air conditioning on?"

I stifled a laugh. "Must be," I said. "Do you come out to Orchard Hollow often?"

"Not at all," Sam admitted. "For obvious reasons."

Right. I was such an idiot. Why would he drive out to the place the woman he was going to marry lived with another man? And, of course, after Stella died, there'd be even less reason for Sam to visit.

"It's a cozy little town you have here."

The server slid two cups onto our table and ran off again. I brought the coffee to my mouth and lowered it immediately. It tasted like a lukewarm puddle. Sam didn't seem to mind since he inhaled half the cup in one gulp.

"It's a nice spot," I agreed. "Though tourist season can be hectic."

"I bet. Is your cafe busy for the most part?"

I nodded. "It does well enough. I only opened it recently, but it's been a lifelong dream of mine."

"Well, you'll have to let me know when you're back in business and I'll make sure to come visit."

Behind his shoulder, Stella swooned and nausea shot up my throat. Why was she behaving like a teenager around this guy? Sure, Sam was attractive and appeared to be in great shape, but for as long as I knew her, my familiar never mentioned anyone except her husband. I wondered if seeing Sam brought back old feelings for her that she may have otherwise tried to suppress.

I checked the clock hanging on the wall anxiously. While I couldn't pinpoint the reason, I felt that we were running out of time with Stella's situation. A shuffle of feet stopped next to me, and I jumped an inch off the chair.

"Miss Addison," Sheriff Romero said, tipping his wide-brimmed hat politely. "Good to see you again."

I wasn't sure why he was acting as though I hadn't just bombarded him with questions about Valerie's alter-ego a day ago. Raising the coffee cup in salute because I was a social train wreck, I ignored Stella's laughter and said, "Hi, Sheriff. This is Sam Collins. He was a friend of Stella's before she moved to Orchard Hollow."

I'd fill Romero in on the relationship between the two later, but I really didn't want to put Sam on the spot right now. Appreciating my candor, he nodded at me, his lips twitching.

"Pleasure to meet you, son," the sheriff said. "Are you visiting for long?"

Sam smiled warmly. "Only for the day. I'm paying my respects to Stella, then back to the city I go."

"Ah, well, enjoy your time here. Make sure you come back when the weather is warmer."

I wanted to tell Sam that the weather was rarely warmer but bit my tongue. "Takeout for the station?" I asked Romero instead.

"Best Sloppy Joes in town," the sheriff answered. He held up a generous paper bag with grease stains soaking its bottom to prove his point. I gagged a little in my mouth. "Actually, I'm glad I ran into you, Miss Addison. I have information on the issue you asked me to look into."

I waved absently in Sam's direction. "It's fine, sheriff. You can tell me what you found on Valerie's fake name in front of Sam. He's been helping me out, so he should hear it too."

"Unless you prefer I leave?" Sam asked.

Next to him, my ghost familiar swooned as though the man offered his heart to a dying saint.

"No need," Romero said. "It isn't all that much, I'm afraid. Nothing on a Catherine Strand came up, but there was a speeding ticket for a Kate Strand a few towns over. Right outside Greenshield."

Brows rising, I knocked my knees together and straightened out my curved back. "Greenshield? That's only a forty-minute drive from us. Do you think it could be Valerie?"

"Perhaps. I tracked the address on the ticket to a rental down by the bay. Same name on the renter's log."

This was much too coincidental to be an actual coincidence. Kate Strand... Catherine Strand... It was too close together. As Romero said, perhaps it was nothing, but what if Valerie was right under our noses the entire time?

I had to check it out.

Stopping myself from bolting right there and then, I flattened my palms out on the table, my index finger playing with the base of the coffee cup. "Do you mind texting me the address?" I asked Romero. When his expression soured, I added, "I promise I will not do anything that could get me into trouble."

"This time," the sheriff mumbled under his thick mustache.

Despite his resignation, he texted me the address. I pulled it up on a map as soon as he left our table and walked out. It was a small cottage in Greenshield, a fishing town near to us. According to the map, I could be there in under an hour if I left immediately.

My fingers danced on the table, a speedy number accentuating my nerves.

"I'll get the bill and we'll head out," Sam suddenly said. "We can get something to eat on the way instead."

Eyeing him suspiciously, I flipped the phone screen around. "You don't have to drive all the way out there with me. You're only in town for the day. You should enjoy the sights."

"I won't enjoy anything knowing that Valerie, the woman who may have caused Stella's death, is out there," Sam argued. "She could be dangerous, Piper. You shouldn't go alone."

He had me there. Normally I'd be messaging Joe

to meet me, but I was beginning to feel terrible about all the times I dragged him out based on a hunch. Now that we were officially dating, I didn't want him to think of me as a basket case chasing leads. He deserved to spend time with the other Piper. The fun Piper that wasn't always knee-deep in murders.

With Stella hot on my heels, I followed Sam to the register and waited for him to pay for our coffees, then out the door. We decided to take the Beetle since I knew how to get to Greenfield faster and his car was parked a hike away. The parking lot in front of the diner was packed again.

My car cooperated for once and I didn't have to be embarrassed about the groaning noises it often resorted to before starting the engine. As I veered out of the lot, my gaze landed on Stella in the rearview mirror. It was no surprise that she was watching Sam as we drove, her eyes never leaving his lips. My heart ached for her.

Stella Rutherford had it bad and there was nothing her dead self could do about it.

CHAPTER 20

The map on my phone's screen froze, the little arrow showing our location stuck in the same spot while we continued forward. Around us, there was nothing but trees. Engine sputtering, I swerved down the winding gravel road leading to the rental cottage Valerie was supposedly staying in.

Nerves wracked my body, the onset of a headache careening from temple to temple.

"Are you sure this is it?" Stella asked. Her first time speaking on the entire drive to Greenshield.

I caught her eyes in the rearview, then pretending to speak to Sam, said, "I know we're on the right road, but does this seem too in the middle of nowhere to you?"

"Not really," Sam answered, staring out the passenger side window. "If I was going to lie low, this would be exactly the type of place I'd pick."

I frowned.

Behind us, Stella made a noise somewhere between a sigh and a grunt, her lips smacking. It made me frown deeper.

"I know you can't talk right now," Stella said, "but he has a point. Sam has a keen sense for people reading. It was his most infuriating trait."

Why did it feel that she meant to say sexy instead of infuriating?

Noticing my glaring, Stella continued yapping. "Do you think he misses me?"

I shifted uncomfortably in the seat, the torn leather of the Beetle catching the fibers of my cardigan. What was up with my familiar? Whatever effect Sam had on her when she was alive was back in full force. I didn't even see her behave this way when we went to see Arthur and he was the love of her life; or so she said. I couldn't figure her out, and it was driving me insane.

One thing was for sure, Stella would keep running her mouth unless I got Sam talking. Turning her question around, I side-eyed the security guard and took the next right turn deeper into the forest. "Do you miss her? Stella, I mean."

While Sam considered my question, I watched the ghost carefully in the mirror. She was grayer than normal, as though whatever was left of her lifeline had finally seeped away.

"Stella was the best thing to ever happen to me," Sam finally said. "She kept me on my toes and never let me get away with anything. It was great while it lasted."

"We sure had fun, didn't we?" Stella asked. Her eyes drifted out the window, knowing she would not receive an answer.

In my chest, my heart jolted. This was too depressing for words.

The road we were on narrowed further and I had to watch the sides of the car to make sure we didn't roll into the drop off on either side. Even though the sun was high above us, it was dark enough that I had to turn on the headlights to see clearly, the trees doing a stellar job of obscuring all light. Somewhere in the depths of the forest, the rustling of wildlife cut the silence.

I closed my fingers over the steering wheel and slowed down, the gravel crunching under the tires as we crept through the musky dark.

"Looks like reception is shot," Sam said.

My eyes floated to my cell on the dashboard, the little arrow signaling our location stuck in the same spot it was in when we entered the forest. The blue line trailing to the cottage remained, so as long as I followed it, we should be pulling up in a few minutes.

And then what?

I had no idea, so instead of freaking out over a plan, I focused my energy on driving. Further in the distance, the low glimmer of a light pierced the dim air, and I slowed even further, the Beetle nearly crawling now. Killing the headlights to avoid giving us away, I rose higher to see past the dashboard. My eyes narrowed on the road. Little by little, we approached our final destination and little by little, I wanted to throw up even more.

"We should probably stop here," Sam instructed.

Nodding, I slowed to a stop and put us in park. Careful not to slam the door, I crawled out of the car and followed Sam down the makeshift road toward what we assumed was the cottage. When we got close enough to see, our eyes adjusting to the low light between the trees, relief flowed through me. It was quickly replaced with a nervous energy I couldn't shake.

Settled between several large oak trees was a small stone cottage. It was very similar in style to the other homes in Greenshield, the fishing village capitalizing on a cozy appearance to draw in tourists, I bet. The cottage was one you might find in a fairytale book, complete with a chimney with smoke pouring out of it, a swinging bench on the wraparound porch, and adorable, rabbit-shaped planters lining the small path leading to the front door.

If we weren't here to stalk someone who may have killed my familiar, I'd be gushing.

Feet crunching the dirt path, I marched for the front door at the same time as Sam grabbed my arm to hold me back. He spun me around to face him. His index finger pressed to his lips. Behind him, Stella's eyes widened until she looked comical.

"Let's not do anything rash," Sam whispered. "We don't know if Valerie is in there, and if she is, if she's alone. We need to be very careful here, so no one gets hurt."

I guessed Sam had the same idea as I did about Stella's friend. Nodding, I slowed my stride and followed behind Sam as he slunk around the building, taking us toward the back of the house. Our bodies stayed in the shadows cast by the sloping roof and we pressed ourselves into the stone, skirting the small building quietly. My feet padded softly as we neared the only window on this side of the cottage.

Quietly, Sam ducked down and crouch-walked under the window to stand on the other side.

I drew in a slow breath and peered in with one eye.

The cabin was lit in a low warm light, painting the small living room in a reddish hue. Not seeing anyone inside, I poked my head out further. On the opposite side of where we stood was a fireplace with small flames dancing inside. Beyond the living room, which was decorated entirely in antiques, stood a tiny kitchen housing a small round table with two chairs tucked in. I noticed movement in my periphery and pressed myself deeper into the stone of the exterior wall.

Stepping out of a darkened hallway was a woman in her early fifties. She wore a thick red sweater and black leggings tucked into a pair of knitted socks. I rolled my eyes up her body to her face, a gasp clogging my throat.

"It's Valerie," I whispered to Sam.

Intrigue flashed over his face and he rose from the crouch he was in to look in the window. "That is definitely her."

As I studied the woman, it occurred to me that she did not resemble a killer. In my experience so far, none of them did. Yet Valerie especially didn't. I wasn't sure how to explain it, but she seemed so...normal.

Wanting to check on Stella, I started to turn from the window when a bright gleam caught my eye. I followed its trajectory to Valerie's wrist and my stomach nearly emptied itself. Pulling Sam's shirt, I tugged him closer to me. "She's wearing Stella's bracelet," I told him.

"The diamond one?"

I swallowed hard. "Yes. That's it without question."

"There's only one way she could have gotten it..."

Sam's words trailed off, but we both knew where he was going. If Valerie was wearing Stella's bracelet, the one she never took off, it could only be because she ripped it off her cold, dead body.

My vision flickered and my balance gave way. I leaned against the cabin's wall, trying to keep from sliding down to the ground. I couldn't believe it. We found Valerie. And we might have found our killer, too.

Reaching for my phone, I realized I had no use for it since there was no service out here, anyway. *We should leave. We should call the sheriff. Or...*

Sam must have been thinking the same thing I was because he said, "I should go talk to her. Maybe if she sees a familiar face, we can get a confession."

"Are you sure? She could be dangerous," I urged.

"It's fine, honestly. I handle people much scarier than Valerie every day at the casino. This is nothing." He glanced around, noting how alone we were in this place. "If I'm not out in ten minutes, take the car and get the hell out, okay?"

I nodded, my heart racing as I watched him walk toward the front door. Deep down, I knew his plan was solid. Sam had much more experience dealing with these types of situations and if things were to go south, I could try to use my magic to help out. It would be easier to do that from out here, where neither he nor Valerie could see me.

I looked down at my hands, smiling at the small sparks of electricity already gathering on them. *Good. At least that's working.*

"I don't like this," Stella said.

I spun around toward her, my hands lit up like a Christmas tree. "He'll be fine," I tried to reassure her. "Sam can handle himself."

"That's not what I mean," the ghost said. "This entire situation feels wrong. Why is Valerie here, of all places? Why kill me then hide out so close to where it happened? And that bracelet, why flaunt it?"

Scratching my jaw, I considered her words. It was a very odd way to behave for someone who murdered her best-friend. Ex-best-friend. It didn't matter. My body slammed to the wall, and I twisted to look inside again. Sam made it in. He stood in front of the kitchen table, facing the window. *To draw attention away from me,* I thought. *Brilliant.*

From this vantage point, I couldn't make out Valerie's face, but by the state of her rigid back, I'd say she wasn't pleased to see the security guard. I pressed my nose to the glass and paused.

My phone was vibrating.

"What the..." I whispered, staring at the screen.

"I thought there's no reception," Stella noted.

I quirked a brow. "There isn't. It could be off and on." Not recognizing the number, I stepped away from the window and picked up the call. "Hello?"

"He...who...calling back."

Reception may have been an exaggeration for this scenario. The call was breaking up so badly I could hardly make anything out.

"Miriam Stolcek. Returning your call...Stella... Valerie..."

"Hi, hello!" I said in a panic. "You're really breaking up. Can I call you back?"

The line crinkled a few times, then the voice returned. "Can you hear me now?"

"Yes," I said, "but I'm not sure for how long."

"I'm returning your call..." Crinkle, crinkle, crinkle. "...about my husband and the casino incident."

My breath got trapped in my chest. Taking a few

more deliberate steps away from the cottage, I said, "Yes, thank you. I'm in a bit of a spot right now. I might lose you."

"That's fine," the woman said. "You mentioned Stella and Valerie in your message. Did you know them?"

"I knew Stella." I glanced toward the cottage. "Not Valerie. Why?"

More static, followed by a heavy intake of breath as the widow collected herself. "They both worked at the casino when Robert was taken from me. If you see Stella, please let her know I think of her often. She was a good friend to my Robbie. Her and that fiancé of hers."

Pulling the phone away from my ear for a moment, I struggled to understand. My eyes searched for Stella, but she was nowhere to be found. "I'm sorry, do you mean Sam?" I asked. "Sam Collins?"

"Yes, that was him! He was the other guard at the casino...good...friend..."

No, no, no! Don't get cut off now! I looked at the screen, seeing the phone flash before the call dropped off. "Damn!"

My fingers worked overtime to call the woman back when a loud, sharp sound tore apart my eardrums. The phone slipped from my hands, falling to the ground. My eyes widened, and I bent to pick it up before rushing toward the front door, heart racing in my chest. I couldn't be one hundred percent sure, but the bang I heard sounded like a gunshot.

And it came from inside the cottage.

CHAPTER
21

The door to the cottage was slightly ajar when I reached it. My pulse thrummed in my veins, making my breath hitch as I pushed my hand to the wood. I stopped. Bringing my ear to the small opening, I listened for signs of a struggle, but it was quieter than a library inside. Fear gripped my body. What happened in there?

Looking over my shoulder, I signaled for Stella to check it out and she vanished instantly. Two seconds later, the ghost reformed before my eyes, panicked.

"You better get in there now!" she screeched.

I started for the door, stopping again. "Do I need my magic?"

"Not right now. But she's not moving. Go, Piper!"

Not wasting any more time, I pushed the door wide open and rushed inside. My hip knocked something over on the way in and it fell to the floor, the sound of metal hitting wood filling the cottage. I didn't bother checking what it was because my attention was elsewhere.

Eyes glued to the two figures on the living room floor, I took a few steps toward them, stopping next to Sam. He crouched beside the couch with a metal object in his hands. The gun I heard.

Turning my head, I looked at the other figure. Valerie's body was unmoving as she lay on her side atop a floral carpet five feet from Sam and me. Her face was turned away from us and I couldn't tell if she was breathing. Beneath her, red, oozing liquid stained the carpet's fibers.

"Is she?" I couldn't finish the sentence.

Sam's eyes bulged. "I'm not sure. She pulled a gun on me," he explained, holding up the pistol in his hands. "I didn't even realize she had it before it was too late. She was going to kill me, Piper. I had to do it."

His ashen face dropped, and his hands shook as he held the gun tighter. Slowly, Sam started to stand up, then sat back down again. "What have I done?"

What *had* he done? I wanted to check on Valerie, but my feet refused to move. I was frozen in time and space, my entire being stuck somewhere between the now and the later. Valerie had to be alive, she just had to be. Because if she wasn't—

I couldn't think of that now. I had to get control of the situation.

Tearing myself away from Sam, I walked toward the body on the floor. The smell of iron permeated my senses as I neared. Separating myself emotionally as best as I could, I crouched down, my trembling hand reaching for Valerie. Carefully, and without stepping in any of the blood, I pressed two fingers to the inside of her wrist, waiting. One second. Two seconds. Her pulse thrummed under my fingers and I breathed out in relief.

"She's alive," I told Sam, though I wasn't sure he could hear me over his freak out session. "But barely. We need to call for help."

Swiveling around, I looked for Stella in the cottage. The ghost was gone again. Why did the infuriating woman keep disappearing when I needed her most? This would go a lot smoother if I had some help.

I turned to Sam, who was still in the same spot I left him. His eyes had narrowed to near slits and his mouth was clenched shut. What was up with him? I mean, sure, he shot someone he used to know, but come on! We needed to act fast here!

As carefully as possible, I turned Valerie over to inspect the wound. I followed the trail of blood to her side, my legs shook violently as I lifted her sweater to see the gaping hole the bullet left behind. Doing the only thing I could think of, I pulled off my scarf and wrapped it around her, putting pressure on the wound to keep it from bleeding. What I wouldn't have given in that moment to know some actual witch magic for a change. I had never felt more useless.

My fingers thrummed with energy and I shook them off; my pointless electric magic was not going to do any good right now.

Suddenly, Valerie moaned, and my entire body relaxed. There was a scuffle behind us as Sam got up. I turned halfway, keeping my eye on both of them at the same time.

"Is she okay?" he asked.

I nodded. "For now, yes. What do we do here? We need to call for help, but we can't leave her alone."

"You go," Sam said. "I can watch over her and make sure she's all right until someone comes for us. There should be a signal further back where we cut off the highway."

Was there one? I tried to think back to when the map froze on my phone and couldn't make the connection. The exit off the highway was a good twenty-minute drive, and that was if I sped to get there. It would be a long haul, but I had to try.

Legs shaking, I stood up slowly, a thought occurring to me as I did. Taking a few steps from Valerie's unconscious body, I zeroed in on Sam. "Do you know a guard named Robert Stolcek?"

"Stolcek?" Sam's forehead creased until he resembled an angry Shar-pei. "Haven't heard that name in a while."

I stopped moving. "So you knew him?"

"Sure did. Poor guy got himself in the middle of a crap situation back at a spot we worked at. Why do you bring him up?"

I bit the inside of my cheek, wondering how much I should share. My gut was telling me to be cautious, and I had no idea why. "His name came up when I was looking for Valerie. Stolcek's widow said the three of you worked together at the casino where he died during a robbery." I tipped my chin toward Valerie. "Stella never mentioned it. Figured I'd see if you knew anything."

"Come to think of it," Sam said, "it happened right around the time I last saw Valerie and Chris. You don't think—"

"That the two of them robbed the casino Valerie worked at? Killed Robert accidentally, then fled into hiding? Maybe."

Did I think that? I wasn't certain. It made sense that it was the reason they disappeared, but the theory didn't quite fit. Why would Valerie bother coming out of the woodwork if there was a chance she could be identified? Getting caught would surely mean jail time for her. Robert Stolcek died because of her and her boyfriend; no judge would let her go free after that.

Then why would she go see Stella, who could easily rat her out?

I was missing something big, and I hated it.

"It was a hit and run, right?" Sam asked, jarring me. "I think I remember it being a truck that got him. I should really go visit Miriam one of these days. It's been too long."

Saliva pooled in my mouth and I clamped my jaw tight, random thoughts buzzing through my brain. A truck and a hit and run. That was way too close for comfort. My sight blurred as I struggled to connect the dots.

"You all right?"

Shivering, I snapped back to reality. "A truck has been following me," I told him. "Tried to run me off the road."

"Whoa. I hope you got the license plate number."

"I didn't," I said, sighing. "And I've been having this weird tingling feeling that Stella's death has a lot to do with a hit and run. Perhaps this was what I was thinking of."

Or that my connection to Stella as a familiar

pushed those thoughts in. I didn't say that part out loud, obviously.

The cabin got colder and a gust of wind blew my hair around. Goosebumps spread over my arms. I ground my teeth together, ready to face Stella upon her return. Finally, the woman had the sense to show up. Turning my back to Sam, I twirled toward my familiar, taken aback by the distress on her face. For a moment, I forgot we weren't alone, words bubbling out of me before I could stop them. "What's wrong?" I asked Stella.

"I went back there again. To the woods and the cliff."

Head tilting, I struggled to make sense of her meaning. I had nothing.

Stella crossed the room, standing inches from me now. Her eyes darted over my shoulder to look at Sam. When she saw him, they darkened with rage. Her cold breath coated my face as she breathed out, "I was there, Piper. I know what happened."

"Wait, what? How? What did you see?"

At my back, Sam murmured, probably asking me if I lost it since I was clearly having a conversation with the air.

"Why don't you ask him how he really got that tooth knocked out?" Stella suggested.

Slower than molasses, I twisted my body so I could

face Sam. What did Stella mean by that? Sam said he got hurt on the job. Didn't he? She couldn't possibly be implying that Sam—

I froze mid-thought. There was no time to dissect what Stella meant. I already knew the answer. I knew it because I was staring down the barrel of a gun and Sam's finger was on the trigger.

CHAPTER 22

"Sam, what's going on?" I asked. A part of me already knew the answer, but hey, a girl had to try. A girl also had to stop getting herself into situations where guns were pointing at her face, but that was a matter for another time.

Gun firmly in hand, Sam gestured with it to the couch. "I really wish I didn't have to do this," he said. "Sit, please. And hands where I can see them."

I didn't know why he cared so much about my hands. I wasn't the one with the weapon here. Careful not to startle the man, who was a second away from ending me, I tiptoed to the couch and slowly lowered down. The cushion sank under my weight and I was swallowed by its velvet fabric instantly. My back strained to stay upright in case I had to run, not that I had any chance of outrunning a bullet.

I glanced at Valerie's body close to my feet. Is that what she tried to do?

Standing next to the gun-wielding maniac was Stella. My familiar was impossible to read on most days, yet right now, I knew exactly what she was thinking.

Screw you, Samuel Collins!

The ghost snarled as Sam tilted the barrel of the gun to point at my heart. "I hope you understand that I don't have a choice in this."

"What happened to Stella?" I asked. I didn't care to hear his explanations for why he decided I didn't deserve to live today. Why he thought the same of Valerie before I walked into the cottage. "You didn't get your tooth knocked out at the casino, did you?"

The security guard flinched.

"He has me to thank for that," Stella barked out. "I used that nasty pearl bracelet he tried to win me back with to punch him. The lying, murdering son of a—"

Gripping the sides of the couch and shifting slightly, I positioned myself so I could see the room clearer while Stella ranted. There was only one way out—the same way I came in—unless I wished to cata-pult myself out the window. An option, but not one I was keen on.

At my feet, Valerie moaned again and Sam jerked the gun in her direction. "Hey!" I yelled to get his attention. "She can't hurt you right now, so knock that off."

The bastard laughed. "Neither can you," he said. He had a good point. "And in case you're wondering, what happened with Stella was an accident."

"How do you accidentally push someone off a cliff?"

"I didn't push her," Sam said. "We argued. She got upset and slipped."

An accusing finger dangled in front of his deceitful face. Stella Rutherford was not buying this story, and neither was I. "Liar!" the ghost shrieked. "I remember everything, Piper. It's like a floodgate opened. I materialized back in the woods again, except this time it was different. The longer I stayed there, the more of my memories came back." She looked at Sam with utter disgust. "He tried to make me help him steal from Arthur. Valerie warned me, but I didn't believe her until Sam showed up. The lying sack of garbage thought I'd actually turn against my husband if he showed up with tacky jewelry and reminisced over old times."

My pulse slowed to a steady beat. While I should have been freaking the heck out, having Stella here kept me level-headed. Not that she could aid me, but simply being near her was enough to keep my head straight. Not making any sudden movements, I leaned into the couch for support. "You didn't know Stella if you thought a bracelet would sway her to betray her husband," I told Sam. Then, remembering the Rutherfords, added, "I mean, they were pearls."

Whatever I said made Sam lose his vigor, and the gun slumped a little in his grasp. Next to him, Stella scoffed, pleased with me for a change.

"How do you know about the bracelet?" Sam asked.

I know a lot more than you think, I wanted to say. I didn't, of course. Telling someone who's pointing the gun at you that you can put them behind bars was not the smartest play. Unfortunately, I had no idea what I should be doing instead.

"Tell him engraving the S for both our names was a cute touch," Stella said. "And that the gaudy thing worked wonderfully in place of brass knuckles when I punched his lying mouth in."

A laugh bubbled out of me; I had to clench my teeth from letting it escape. Even in a time such as this, Stella was herself. A force to be reckoned with. I couldn't believe the slimeball with the gun in front of me was the reason she wasn't alive anymore. The thought enraged me. All I wanted was to unleash my magic on the murdering creep. I couldn't do that, though. Not only because I wasn't sure if my magic would even work, but because I needed to get Sam to confess to everything. If I was going to die today, I'd take Stella's killer down with me.

For a brief moment, Sam's eyes darted away and I took my chance. An inch at a time, I stretched my arm into the back pocket of my pants and pulled out my cell phone. I sat it on the couch behind me, out of Sam's line of sight. When the security guard walked to the window to shut the curtains, I quickly turned on the voice memo app and pressed record.

"Why Stella?" I asked. "Why not another casino?"

Sam tugged at the curtain again to make sure no one from outside could see in. He walked slowly, deliberately, and I knew immediately that he had no intention of letting me walk out of here alive. My eyes crept downward to Valerie's body, her chest rising and falling. Neither of us would survive him.

"She had an in," Sam said finally. His lips peeled back to a sneer. "And..."

I frowned. "And you thought she still had feelings for you and would drop her life in a heartbeat if you came calling."

"As if I would," Stella sniped.

"You didn't count on her actually being too in love with Arthur to go for it, though," I said. "Did you ever chase her down here like you told me or was that a lie, too?"

The guard bristled, then used the barrel of the gun to scratch under his chin. "Not a lie. She didn't want anything to do with me then."

"Why try again?"

"For the money," Sam said, as if it was the most obvious answer in the world. "The Rutherford name was failing, Arthur and that fraud of a partner of his were on their last legs. I thought if I offered Stella a way out, and the means to get it, she'd see reason."

Not far from him, I noticed Stella's ghostly shape float by. Her fingers reached for Sam's throat and when she floated through him, the guard shivered. Pleased, Stella did it again, a smirk on her pursed lips. My familiar was sure enjoying herself at all the wrong moments. Tearing my focus away from her, I looked at Sam. His posture slumped a bit but his eyes were sharp and trained directly on me. "Stella would never betray Arthur," I told him. "She loved him."

"Yes, I got that part."

"Ask him why he killed Chris," Stella noted.

I twisted my body closer to her as she hovered over Valerie, checking on the woman when I couldn't. "Christopher Meadow's death wasn't an accident either," I said.

"You really are quite clever," Sam mused. "I can see why Stella and you were friends."

Are *friends, you dimwit.*

I shimmied, crossing my arms to keep my heart in check while it pounded against my ribcage. For the first time, I didn't have a plan. The cottage was quite literally in the middle of nowhere. I had no reception and no way out and my only help was a dead woman with a grudge.

I was in it deep and I knew it.

"So what happened? Did Valerie and Chris figure out your plan and you had to handle them the way you handled Stella?" It didn't quite add up. Why did those two disappear all those years ago? I narrowed my eyes at Sam. "What really happened to Robert Stolcek?"

The guard waved the gun around as he spoke, and my muscles tensed. "I should have known that name would come back to haunt me."

"That's not the only thing that's going to haunt you," Stella hissed between clenched teeth. "When Valerie came to warn me, she told me they'd been running from Sam for years. That he's the one that organized the casino robbery; that he ran over the guard. He told them he'd pin it all on her and Chris, so they ran. She thought no one would believe the two of them over someone like Sam."

Shadows crept across Stella's eyes. I didn't know if

ghosts could cry, but I was certain I saw the glimmer of a tear when she whispered, "I would have believed them."

Sam stalked the room, covering every inch as he padded from the open kitchen to the window, then back again. A bead of sweat rolled down his cheek, and he swiped at it angrily. The guard was getting agitated. I was running out of time.

Spinning on his heels, he turned to me. "It doesn't matter what happened to Stolcek. He shouldn't have gotten himself so involved," he huffed out. "You'd think he was on the force, that guy. I told him a million times to keep his nose to the ground. Clock in, clock out. Why he didn't wasn't my problem."

"So you killed him for it?"

"I did no such thing!" Sam exclaimed. "He literally jumped in front of the truck. I didn't even see the guy before it was too late."

Truck... My brain worked overtime to connect the pieces. I was willing to bet that the car Sam had conveniently parked too far away today was a truck. Likely the same one that killed Robert and tried to run me off the road. What a piece of work.

He started to pace again, Stella following his steps, fumes rising from her. I leaned on my elbows and checked on Valerie. She was breathing, but slower. I had to hurry and think of a way out of this mess, for both our sakes. The shine of diamonds caught my eye as Valerie inhaled a ragged breath. There was one thing I didn't understand. When Sam stopped moving, I caught his gaze in mine. "Why did Valerie have Stella's diamonds?"

"Good catch," Sam said, walking to Valerie's body. He bent down, the gun pointing at me, and snatched the bracelet off her wrist. A red mark spread over her bronze skin. Same as Stella's. "I should probably take back what's mine since Val didn't hold up her end of the deal."

"You used it to pay her off? For what?"

"Staying quiet, obviously," Stella murmured in my ear. "He gave her the bracelet to make her and Chris disappear again. It wasn't bad enough the last time the three worked together, Sam turned against them; now he was blackmailing them to keep their mouths shut about what he did to me."

"But how did he find them in the first place? I thought Valerie and Chris were hiding out after what happened to Robert?"

Sam's eyes narrowed on me. "Who are you talking to?"

"No one," I said and waited for Stella to finish speaking.

The ghost frowned so deep, I almost saw lines on her porcelain face. "Sam tracked them down somehow," she said. "Then came for me. The day it happened, he called me out of the blue. Said he was in town and wanted to meet up and I fell for it. We met on the trails. That's when he switched his game, the bastard."

"What happened on those trails, Sam?" I asked the guard. "Your plan to woo Stella didn't work so well, did it? She met you there to ask you to leave, didn't she?"

Neck blotchy and red, Sam crossed from the kitchen to the couch, the gun up in the air once more. "How do you know all this? Only Stella knew what happened that day," he shrieked. "She shouldn't have turned me down. All she had to do was go along with the plan. Val and Chris would have come around too if she agreed to it, I know it. But no, Stella had to be the self-righteous woman she always was. If she didn't threaten to turn me in, everything would be different."

"I don't think that's true," I breathed out. I pointed to his missing front tooth. "Stella wants you to know she enjoyed that."

Sam's face dropped, and he stutter stepped away from me, his eyes darting around the empty room. "Stella wants me to what?"

Good, I thought. *Keep going. Get him confused, then use your magic to knock him out. You can do this.*

The plan was working; I could feel the air change

as Stella floated toward Sam, helping me set the atmosphere. For the first time, the ghost and I were connected in a way we hadn't been before. She knew what I wanted to do without me saying a word. Stella's gray figure rushed into Sam, materializing behind him.

The guard shivered and kicked his left leg out in a panic. His mouth hung open as he continued to search the room for the woman he would never see. I was so entranced by my familiar's performance, I didn't concentrate hard enough. Which was how I didn't notice what happened next before it was too late.

As Stella readied to rush her ex-fiancé, he twirled in a half-circle. His legs planted firmly on the ground as he faced me. "Screw this," was the last thing Sam said before he raised his arm and fired a bullet aimed straight for me.

CHAPTER 23

Nothing is quite as terrifying as the sound of a gun firing. Especially when that gun is aimed at your face. When Sam loosened a shot, meaning to kill me, I could only think of one thing. I'm glad Stella is here with me.

There was no time to think, to even breathe, really. The bullet zoomed through the air too fast for any rational decisions. My first instinct was to throw my hands up to stop the impact. A foolish idea.

Or was it?

As my palms pushed out, the magic living inside me burst from my skin. It swirled around my fingers, its blue electric glow casting brightness on my face and in the space between me and the incoming bullet.

Time slowed.

I wasn't sure how, but the bullet seemed to float rather than burst forward at an impossible speed.

Gathering more of my magic, I searched for guidance I wasn't sure would be there. At the rear of my mind, a tingle of a thought appeared, and I clung to it for dear life. Memories of the nightmare I had returned to me in flashes.

Dark rooms. Screaming. Burning flames.

I pictured the dream as though it were a memory, imagining the terrifying place I knew couldn't truly exist. As I did, the magic on my hands grew, blinding me with its power. Arms stretching outward, I continued to see the nightmare realm, feeding the image into my magic. A gasp burst from my lips. In the space between the bullet and me, the air rippled. It was nothing at first, a flutter. A loose thought. Then it solidified and grew larger, and I recognized immediately. It was the same rip in the air I'd seen several times before. Except this time, I was the one creating it.

"What in the name of coffee?" I whispered as the rip expanded.

Inside it, a flash of movement caused me to tip backward. My shoulders hit the couch cushion, and I pressed myself into it, hoping it would swallow me whole before my own magic destroyed me. I watched with my mouth agape as the rip grew and grew and grew.

A moment later, the bullet appeared, quickly disappearing as it shot into the rip I created. I blinked rapidly. When the bullet tore its way into whatever space in time I opened, the rip shimmered, a bright blue light emanating from it and lighting up the entire cottage in its glare. The house rumbled, the ground beneath our feet vibrating. I wrapped my fingers over the side of the couch and tried to find Stella in the room. I couldn't see anything from the glow of my magic.

A second went by, then another. Then the rip closed in on itself and the light vanished. As though nothing happened at all.

Except it did.

My racing heart was proof it.

"What the hell was that?" roared Sam from the edge between the kitchen and living room. The gun was still in his hand, smoking. "What did you do?"

I shook my head because I honestly had no idea. Eyes ducking to my hands, I saw no hint of the magic that was there moments ago. My muscles tensed and my chest constricted. A gargantuan knot formed in my throat.

Somewhere not too far from me, Sam continued to bellow. "What are you?"

"Piper, watch out!"

Stella's warning shot through the air faster than the bullet. I threw my head up in time to see Sam barrel his muscular body toward me. His chest slammed into mine and pushed me into the couch. The couch's arm hit my shoulder blades, and I winced as a hollow pain shot down my body. We tumbled to the floor, our bodies entwined.

I tried to regain control, but Sam was so much stronger. His body twisted, and he pinned me down, his thighs digging into my hips to hold me in place. Hands reaching out, he circled his thick fingers around my throat.

Dots swarmed my vision.

My chest heaved as I tried to breathe, but my lungs refused to expand. A few feet from me, Valerie's body lay in a helpless heap. Tears streamed down my face as I fought for my life. This couldn't be how it ended. I wasn't done yet. I wasn't ready. I blinked away my failing vision.

Is this how Stella felt before she died?

Above me, Sam's face came into focus, only to blur again. My legs kicked out maniacally under him and he pressed all his weight down to hold me in place. I wanted to scream, but no sound came out. Any longer and Sam would snap my neck in two.

A sting of cold air brushed against my wrist.

Shivers tripped down my spine. Fighting through tears, I snaked my eyes to the side and my heart pitter-pattered. *Stella.* The ghost was on her knees, her face so close that chills racked my body. Though that could have been death coming to claim me. Stella's mouth moved, but I couldn't make out her words. The world around me spun in speedy circles. Realizing I couldn't understand her, she stretched her hand out and pointed to my limp fingers. Continuing to reach for me, Stella hovered her palm an inch above mine, nodding for me to do something.

What?

The ghost pointed again, her expression desperate. I followed her glazed eyes to my hand, where her fingers lingered. Did she want to hold my hand in my final moments? Was this Stella's way of comforting me as I went?

No, that couldn't be it. Surely not.

Stella's lips parted wide and though I couldn't hear her, I assumed she was screaming at me. Her hand jerked up and down, getting my attention. I focused my eyes long enough to laser in on my own fingers. They were lit up bright blue with magic.

Following Stella's queue, I struggled against my failing body to stretch my fingers toward hers. I didn't know what I would do once I got there. All I wanted was to be near someone I loved as I took my last breath. Arm shaking violently, I let my fingers graze hers. Frigid cold slashed my skin as Stella's ghostly hand touched mine. Her lips twitched, a sneer tugging at them.

This time, when she grabbed my arm, I felt it.

Shock thrummed through me at the touch. How was I able to feel Stella's skin? Wait, how did Stella have skin at all?

Questions flooded my mind, and I tucked them away. There was no point figuring them out now. Stella yanked at my hand and my body jerked to the side involuntarily. The movement shocked Sam for a brief moment and he pulled away, giving Stella enough space to slip in between us. As she did, my body convulsed.

Suddenly, I wasn't myself anymore, at least, I wasn't only me. As Stella's body laid atop me, it was as though we joined. I wore the ghost like a shield. Like second skin. Stella raised her arms and my own arms shot up. Above me, Sam's brow furrowed in confusion as he tried to understand what was happening.

Together, Stella and I shoved him with our hands and feet. Whatever power the ghost had, fed into my magic. Electric sparks exploded around us and I sucked in a much needed breath while watching Sam catapult away from me. He flew across the living room as though he weighed nothing, his back slamming into the window I spied through earlier. Glass shattered under his weight and Sam grunted, dropping to the floor lifelessly. Pieces of window glass fell around him in piles.

My upper body shot up, and I coughed so hard my chest hurt. Every inch of me felt like it was on fire as I took in breath after breath. To my right, Stella hovered silently. I breathed in again and sighed. Sweet, delicious oxygen.

Finally able to stand, I rose to my feet, my ankles buckling inward slightly.

"What was that?" I asked the ghost.

She shrugged. "An experiment."

"Do I even want to know what you mean by that?"

"Probably not," Stella replied. "Let's say that I wanted to see how deep your underworld powers run."

My thighs pressed together as I worked to stay upright. "And?"

"Deep. Very, very deep."

Ripping myself away from the cryptic ghost, I looked toward the window and Sam's crumpled body. His chest rose slightly; I was ashamed to admit the disappointment that flashed through me briefly, knowing he was alive. I looked around the room, then walked as fast as I could manage in this frail state to the kitchen. Picking up an apron with some hefty looking strings, I marched toward Sam. At first, I kept my distance, but a job was a job and there was no one else to do it but me.

Careful not to wake the sleeping killer, I knelt beside him and did my best to tie his hands with the apron, making sure to add extra knots to my work. When I finished, I snaked the apron around the radiator Sam lay next to and gave that a good tie as well. I hoped it would hold.

With Sam secure—perhaps—I rushed toward Valerie. The woman was alive, thank the coffee gods. "Stay here and come get me if she's in trouble," I told Stella.

"Where are you going?"

Digging for my phone in between the ruffled couch cushions, I clicked a button to end the recording, my face crumbling. "I'm going to do what I should have done before coming here," I said, limping out the door. "I'm going to call the sheriff."

CHAPTER 24

I t took the sheriff under an hour to meet me at the highway exit and he had the entire cavalry follow him. Flashing lights lit up the exit as the cars drove through. Most passed right by me as I stood waiting on the shoulder, but one pulled over, Sheriff Romero stepping out to greet me. His bushy brows drawn low on his forehead, his expression somewhere between impressed and concerned.

"Well, this took quite a turn," the sheriff said as he approached me.

I let out a half-hearted chuckle. "It always seems to. The cottage is a few miles up that road. Your guys won't be able to miss it."

"You mentioned both victims needing medical attention?"

"One victim," I corrected him. "The other one, the one tied up, killed Stella Rutherford and Robert Stolcek ten years ago. And Christopher Meadow, though I have no proof of that. He never confirmed that one."

Reaching into my back pocket, I pulled out my cell phone and handed it to the sheriff. "There's a recording on there you'll want to hear," I said. "But I need the phone back."

"I'll have someone pull the recording and drop this off for you this evening," Romero said, nodding. "So you finally solved it."

Shoulders slumped, I rubbed my blood-shot eyes until they hurt. Another siren blew out my eardrums as an ambulance veered off the highway and headed in the direction of the cottage. I slumped in relief. Hopefully, they'd be able to help Valerie before it was too late. In the time I spent waiting, Stella popped in and out, keeping me abreast of her condition. Each time she showed up, I exhaled a little deeper. Though not only because of Valerie's health.

Stella got her memories back. She knew what happened to her and got her closure. I didn't know much about the afterlife, but everything I'd read thus far implied that once a ghost closes off all unfinished business, they're out of here. Passing over. Moving into the light. Whatever you want to call it.

Yet Stella stayed.

My happiness at seeing her each time made my stomach twist into knots. I wasn't ready to let her go and if I was honest, I didn't think I ever would be. Stella wasn't just a familiar, she was my best friend; she was family.

Blowing out a fluttering breath, I looked at the sheriff. "You should know, I didn't exactly handle the situation in the most natural way," I revealed. "If Sam starts talking about magic and blue lights, we might have a problem."

"I'll handle it," Romero said. "You need to get home and rest. Speaking of..."

The screech of tires coming to an abrupt stop pulled me away from the sheriff. I turned to look over my shoulder as another vehicle pulled up next to us. I instantly recognized it. Excitement rushed through me as Joe put his car in park and climbed out. He walked toward me, his muscular legs closing the distance in a few long strides. Not looking at the sheriff, Joe opened his arms, and I crashed into him, my face pressing into his rock-hard chest.

As Joe cradled me to him, I saw Stella appear briefly behind him. The ghost flashed her pearly white teeth and winked before vanishing again.

I smiled. *We did it, Stella. We actually freaking did it.*

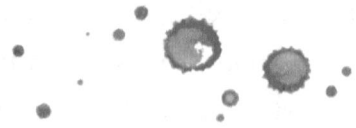

The sound of crackling burning wood worked its way through the house, coating the farmhouse in a blanket of warmth. Outside, wind rustled the trees and I could hear the branches knock against the roof's shingles. I sipped my drink slowly, the taste of cinnamon on my tingling tongue.

Bringing an off the shoulder navy sweater to myself, I tilted my head and inspected it in the floor-length mirror. "How about this one?"

"It's perfect," Stella said, "for a funeral."

Sticking my tongue at her, I walked back to the closet to pick out another outfit. Joe was going to be here any minute, and I was running behind. As per usual. This would be our second date where once again, he wouldn't tell me what he had planned. One of these days, I'd have to break it to the man that surprises were not my favorite thing. Though I did love seeing him try to impress me.

Stella reached a hand into the closet and yanked

out a black dress, tossing it on the bed. "This one," she said triumphantly.

"You're getting eerily good at that."

It was true, my familiar had become exceptionally great at interacting with the living world since the incident in the cottage. We still couldn't explain exactly what happened there, nor did we know why Stella was around, despite having her memories back and her killer behind bars. I thought it was because she was tied to me as a familiar. Joe's theory was that it had something to do with my Hades magic. Stella simply said that being here was more fun than being anywhere else.

Tiny rodent feet scurried across the bedroom floor behind me. My eyes snapped to the raccoon as he wrapped his tiny fingers around my mug and dragged it under the bed.

Harry Houdini had no theories at all.

I wasn't too eager to solve the mystery of why my familiar was hanging about; I was simply happy she was here. And that she was helping me get ready because Stella Rutherford was the walking definition of put together. Well, the floating definition.

Cramming myself into the incredibly tight dress she picked out, I lifted my hair off my shoulders and gazed in the mirror.

"He won't know what hit him," Stella said from behind me.

I grinned widely. "Thank you," I said. Catching a glimpse of her in the reflection, I dropped my hair, letting it fall down in tight, red ringlets. "How are you feeling today?"

"Piper, please, stop," the ghost said, shooing me off.

"I'm only checking in. You've been through a lot."

Ignoring me, the ghost disappeared, then popped up again next to the vanity table. Her hand dug into the open jewelry box and she yanked out a pearl necklace, placing it on the table. "Try these, they might work," she said.

"They're pearls," I answered, chuckling.

"Sometimes," Stella said, "pearls are exactly what one needs."

With that one sentence, Stella said more than she had since the sheriff hauled Sam off in handcuffs. Her ex-fiancé, the man who murdered her, was currently awaiting trial in King City. There was no evidence to link him to Christopher's death, but the recording I had made sure he'd go down for at least two murders; Stella's and Robert's. That and the blood on the pearl bracelet leading back to Sam's DNA made sure he was never going to see the outside of a jail cell again.

It was all thanks to a pearl bracelet.

Closing the distance between myself and Stella, I

picked up the necklace and put it on. As I did, my fingers brushed against hers and we both shivered. Stella's eyes caught mine. "Boundaries, Piper. We discussed this."

I laughed and wiggled my fingers at her tauntingly. At that, the ghost flipped her long ponytail in my face, the tips of her shiny hair slapping me across the nose. I sneezed, which made Stella burst out laughing. Soon, the two of us were cackling like idiots, the farmhouse shaking with our senseless joy. I wondered if Gran could see me now. She'd be glad to know of the small place I carved for myself here in Orchard Hollow. My eyes darted down to the vintage watch she gave me. "Shoot! I better hurry up."

It turned out there was no more time left. A knock on the downstairs door sent me into a fast-paced race to the finish line. I dabbed on a swipe of lipstick, wrestled my mug away from Harry's grubby paws, threw on a pair of red heels, and flew down the stairs.

Skipping the last step, I miraculously didn't break a leg and was rushing for the door when Stella appeared next to it. She looked me up and down approvingly. "I meant it," the ghost said. "You look brilliant."

Stella vanished as quickly as she appeared, leaving me to greet Joe. My heart raced in my chest. I swiped at the rear of my neck, hoping that I could keep my nerves at bay long enough to stop from sweating through my dress. Reaching for my coat, I tossed it over my arm and opened the door. "Hey, you're—" My teeth clamped shut as I took in the woman standing on the front porch. "Mom?"

"Hi, honey," Sylvie Addison said. "Miss me?"

My mouth hung open, jaw dusting the threshold. "What are you doing here?"

Pushing past me, my mother waltzed into the farmhouse, the wind blowing in stray leaves behind her. I kicked them out with my foot and shut the door. Then chased after her. As I did, Sylvie twirled around dramatically, her long red hair flowing as though she were underwater. "I don't have much time to explain," she said. "You're in danger. We must act quickly or the entire world will pay the price."

There was another knock on the door, Joe finally showing up, but I couldn't bring myself to open it. My mother, the woman who abandoned me all those years ago, was back. And as in standard Sylvie fashion, she brought trouble with her. I looked down at my dress, sighing. This was about to get very interesting.

APPLE SPICED LATTE

Ingredients:

2 shots espresso

1 cup milk

3 tbsp apple spice syrup

2 tsp vanilla extract

Honey to taste

Dash of ground cinnamon

Instructions:

1. Combine apple spice syrup and espresso in a mug.

2. Steam milk over stovetop until just below boiling.

3. Pour milk over syrup and espresso, mix.

4. Add vanilla extract and honey.

5. Sprinkle cinnamon to taste.

ABOUT THE AUTHOR

A.N. Sage is a bestselling, award-winning author of mystery and fantasy novels. She has spent most of her life waiting to meet a witch, vampire, or at least get haunted by a ghost. In between failed seances and many questionable outfit choices, she has developed a keen eye for the extra-ordinary.

A.N. spends her free time reading and binge-watching television shows in her pajamas. Currently, she resides in Toronto, Canada with her husband who is not a creature of the night and their daughter who just might be.

A.N. Sage is a Scorpio and a massive advocate of leggings for pants.

For more books and updates:
www.ansage.ca

Exclusive stories and content:
reamstories.com/ansagewrites

Connect on social media:

Facebook Group:

facebook.com/groups/945090619339423/

Instagram:

instagram.com/a.n.sage/

TikTok:

tiktok.com/@ansagewrites

YouTube:

youtube.com/c/ANSageWrites

www.ingramcontent.com/pod-product-compliance
Lightning Source LLC
Chambersburg PA
CBHW020125120726
47903CB00007B/2103